FIGHT LIKE A GIRL

FIGHT LIKE A GIRL

SHEENA KAMAL

a novel

PENGUIN TEEN

an imprint of Penguin Random House Canada Young Readers,
a division of Penguin Random House of Canada Limited

Published in hardcover by Penguin Teen, 2020
Published in this edition, 2022

1 2 3 4 5 6 7 8 9 10

Manufactured in Canada

Library and Archives Canada Cataloguing in Publication

Title: Fight like a girl / Sheena Kamal.
Names: Kamal, Sheena, author.
Description: Previously published: Toronto: Penguin Teen, 2020.
Identifiers: Canadiana 20200181955 | ISBN 9780735265578 (softcover)
Classification: LCC PS8621.A477 F54 2022 | DDC jC813/.6—dc23

Library of Congress Control Number: 2020951524

www.penguinrandomhouse.ca

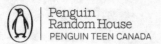

Penguin
Random House
PENGUIN TEEN CANADA

What comes back to you:

It was a dark, rainy night.
There was no moon out.

A story that ends with a thud.

Your father's face.

A shadow in the woods.

A slide into a nightmare.

one

I know that people don't like going to funerals, but this is something else. There's almost nobody here for Dad's cremation service. Some distant relatives, a few of Ma's colleagues and a handful of acquaintances. Whose acquaintances, I have no idea. I've never seen these people before in my life.

Dad's rum shop friends couldn't even peel themselves off their barstools long enough to show up in the afternoon?

What the what.

Somehow, in the middle of the service, Ma senses my mind wandering and sends me a glare that could cut a lesser person with its sharpness. But I'm used to her stabby looks, so it just comes as a warning to sit there and behave, and fold my hands in my lap, and pretend that I like to wear a dress for some reason.

I tried to get away with my black jeans that show off the thick muscles in my legs, but I got a good old Caribbean slap upside the head for that. Ma wasn't having any of it today, of all days. When she was about to say goodbye to the love of her life (gag).

As the service drags on, I should one hundred percent be thinking about my dad and how he died, but I can't bring myself to do it. What I do instead is replay the disastrous events of my last fight. I guess I look dazed because Ma pinches my arm and mutters, "Trisha, don't make me break something over your head, girl. Have some respect!"

Now I *have* to pay attention because her nails are sharper than her looks and if she threatens to break something over my head, you know she will throw down in front of all these people without a care in the world.

Alright, fine.

I focus on the pundit singing religious songs that nobody understands. Finally, after he does the bare minimum to collect his fee, a few people get up to say nice things about Dad and, whoo boy, is it slim pickings up in here! Until Ma gets fed up and makes her way up to give a heartfelt speech about how they met blah blah, how much she loved him et cetera, how long until this is over?

I glance around the room and see "diversity" because this is Toronto, after all, and "diversity" is what it's all about. I mean look at all the assorted *Degrassi* kids, and that was even before Drake came along. We have everybody in Toronto. But in this room, let's be honest, we mostly have Trinidadians and Pammy. And, except for one nice old man who looks like he got lost on the way to the grocery store, the majority are women.

The curse of my life. Trinidadian women. One in particular.

Ma is watching me again and I can tell she's thinking about a slap. I can't really blame her. I'm very trying on her nerves and she's had it rough, my ma. Not that you would know by looking at her.

Rule number one of being a woman from Trinidad: be hella fierce.

I'm not kidding, people. This is the rule. Not only will people expect you to be educated, have a job and provide, you must also have it in you to be an all-round queen. Look after whatever stray children happen to wander your way. Drop everything and whip up some roti on a whim. Plus, you will be fetishized like crazy and you need to be prepared for the sexual energy random assholes will want you to expend whenever a bass line pulses through your prodigious hips. Courtesy of the grand bacchanalia that is Trinidad Carnival, people will look at you and imagine you in barely-there sparkling costumes with your tits out and your ass exposed to the warm sunshine, shaking and backing back on whatever sweaty crotch just so happens to be around for a well-timed jook.

Well, what about the men? (Some people might ask this. Idiots, mostly.)

Well, what about them? The men, they don't matter. Not one bit. Looking around this sad excuse for a funeral, they're not even here. They're good for a poke in the night—two sapodilla and a nine-inch banana, as the calypso goes—but not much more than that. I've got hordes of useless uncles and semi-uncles (and people I'm just supposed to call uncle even though we're not related) to prove my point. What they do best is disappear. Even when they're right in front of you, they're somewhere else. Forever playing cards in the rum shops of their minds.

It's the women that stay.

They're with you even when they're not around. They give you pieces of their souls, jagged pointy things, and you can never give them back, no matter how much you want to. No matter how much these pieces cut you and make you bleed for them, over and over.

I have to tell you something.

The women of my family are both warriors and witches. Creatures of the night, vampires that haunt the dreams of Caribbean children, soucouyants who will suck the life right out of you and burn you with our flames.

I first begin to suspect this about my family after Mr. Abdi gives me a book about a soucouyant living in my hood. Fiction, he says. Yeah, right. Like women who take everything you have and keep wanting more could ever be some made-up shit in the pages of a book.

Another pinch from Ma tells me the service is finally over.

Mourners trail out and some of them even make it to our townhouse co-op in the east end of Toronto for the food part, which is probably what lured them to the service in the first place. They walk into the front door, past the boiler room, which we call the basement, and up the stairs to where the living room, dining room and kitchen are. There's another floor with the bedrooms, but nobody goes up there to poke around because the food is laid out on the dining room table. People practically eat and run, muttering their condolences, and we try to find something new to say every time.

It's an ordeal, but we do our best.

We are the saddest people you ever saw, but after everyone leaves our house with their bellies full of dhalpuri, curry channa and sahina, all of a sudden it feels different somehow. Lighter. Like how my arms feel at the gym after Kru makes me punch with weights for what seems like hours. Like they could float away.

I walk into the kitchen and I feel this airiness about Ma. The grief she should feel over my father's death is suddenly somewhere in the wind, far away from here. Maybe her sadness joined him at a nearby rum shop—no doubt where his spirit flew when it exited his mutilated body. Even in her black dress, her face bare of makeup, her hair pulled tight into a bun, she's light itself in this moment.

Which is weird, right?

And it's like I'm waking up from a dream. I see the smile that my mother gives to my aunty Kavita. Pammy, our next-door neighbor, comes in and grins at them both. A pit of dread opens up inside me because it's like I'm not even there and they're sharing something I SHOULD NOT be seeing. Pammy's inclusion in whatever's happening here shocks me. We are the witchiest of warriors if we're starting to corrupt the white people in the neighborhood, too.

Make them into killers, like us.

one month earlier

two

In the warehouse district on the east side of the city, the Muay Thai gym I train at is tucked between two underground sweatshops that pretend in the daytime they're legit clothing manufacturers. The ring has seen better days—

duct tape on the floor, the ropes *and* the posts

—but the mats aren't revolting and the gear is disinfected at least once a week.

There isn't much more you can ask for, really. Kru does his best, but he's pretty busy, what with his plans to expand across the city and spread the joy of connecting shinbone to ribs. Fist to chin. Knee to solar plexus. Elbow to . . . you get it.

We call each other gladiators because we go out and fight for reasons beyond us. Reasons that nobody else can understand if you're not part of it. We don't even understand it, not really. Nobody is from here, or from Thailand, even, the birthplace of our sport, Muay Thai. Some people call us *nak muay farang*—foreign boxers. We're from a couple dozen other countries at least, the knot at the center of Canada's cultural mosaic, where everybody is from somewhere else.

Our origin stories are irrelevant here, because we all want the same thing.

That rush.

The Art of Eight Limbs, the Thai words that stutter off our tongues. They don't sound right, even to us, but none of that matters. Not really. As long as we pay our respects, we get a pass to train. To fight.

I'm in the ring right now.

I do my Wai Kru, the pre-fight dance, and bow to my Filipino coach, who was made Kru ten years ago in Thailand, the only place where it matters. The mecca of warriors like us, in our bright shorts and with our hard bodies. Kru is there in my corner and our team is behind him, cheering. He gives me that look, the one that says *You got this, Lucky*, and steps back. The rest of the team melts away and it's just me and her. My opponent. There's this calm that comes over me, this peace. I see the fierce look in her eyes but I make my own go soft so I can see her whole body, trying to sense her weakness.

Then one of us moves, and it begins. A dance. Brutal, but beautiful, too.

When it's all over, after a left hook catches me at the precise spot that my headgear shifted, plowing through my temple and leaving me face down on the bloody mat, I sit alone on a bench in the locker room of my gym, smelling of sweat and tangy Thai liniment. After all the consolation hugs and smacks on the back, my team has left me alone. Which is how I like it best.

A fallen gladiator. Beaten but not defeated.

Undoing my wrist wraps. Pulling off my compression sleeves. Taking the braid out of my hair. I step into the shower and feel the heat of the water sear the pain away and I feel fresh. I forget that my dad is arriving from Trinidad tomorrow, for about a month (as usual), bringing with him a suitcase full of frozen food, made by the hands of women I've never met, blood connections who will never stop cooking for other people until the day they die. Food parcelled out in little baggies just so and wrapped up tight for the trip. Frozen coconut water in plastic Coke liter bottles, sealed with duct tape. There will also be tamarind balls for me, because he knows how much I love them.

That's the only thing he knows about me.

He brings nothing for Ma, nothing but his fists.

three

I don't go with Ma to pick Dad up from the airport because she usually does that alone. Dad never talks about anything interesting anyway, and he definitely doesn't talk about his life back in Trinidad. So what I know about Trinidad isn't much. To tell you the truth, my knowledge about the island my parents were born on could probably fit in an A-cup sparkly Carnival bra with tassels.

This is the whole of it: When Columbus discovered Trinidad, he saw three big hills and thought of a trinity, an inverted triangle that his fellow Europeans could fuck until the Amerindians were gone and they were free to populate their sugar cane plantations with slaves. When slavery was abolished, the need for sugar was still there, so they took indentured laborers from India who lived and worked like slaves for years, though you'll never get a coolie today who'll admit that their people were actual coolies.

Like there's something wrong with being poor and without better options.

So you have to get on a boat and lose your identity, your culture? So you were led astray by false promises? That shit happens. Get over it. Everything I learned about Trinidad I learned from Ma, and she's never had any time for history lessons, what with her long shifts at the hospital and all the effort she spends trying to make my father happy.

Now that Dad's here, I can't wait to get out of the house. Ma, too, it seems. We're at the mall, getting a dress for my graduation ceremony, which will happen in the fall.

"Stand up straight," Ma says, smacking me upside the head with her open palm. The usual. "What are you, a child? Sometimes I think you're seventeen going on twelve."

"Ow," I say, even though I don't mind. The insult or the smack. This is what Amanda from the gym calls a love tap. Her family is from Jamaica, so she's well familiar with the Caribbean style of love.

The store is filled with dresses, not someplace I usually go, but Ma has the money now, so we're buying the dress now. Not off the sale rack, because this is a special occasion. My first full-price dress. A milestone as important to her as my graduation, which is waaay off in the future—

So why are we here exactly, Ma?

—but I can't think about that now because I'm trying to find my balance in something a five-year-old at a princess party wouldn't look out of place in. I stare at myself in the mirror, my muscular shoulders and thighs ruining the drape of pink she's chosen for me.

"You are so dark," she says softly, as though this is a crime.

16

Her expression in the mirror is one of pity, because she is fair and she thought her daughter would be, too. But I'm not. I look like my dad.

Once we get the dress, Ma's in a better mood. She even takes me for lunch, but she can't resist reminding me that there's enough food at home. We eat tacos at the mall food court and I try to forget what she said about my skin. Other people sometimes comment on it, especially when they see me and Ma standing together, but she doesn't usually. I think maybe it reminds her too much of Dad.

After the mall, I ask her to drop me off at the gym. She's probably feeling guilty about the "you're so dark" thing, so she does.

"Trish, you know you're beautiful to me, right?" she says, when she pulls into the gym parking lot.

"Ma."

She ruffles my hair. "You are. Go have fun."

Finally, she lets me out of the car so that I can work up a decent sweat and try to forget about how pink dresses look on my dark skin. Plus, I don't really like being at the house when Dad is around. I think Ma knows it, too.

Whoever said *The blacker the berry, the sweeter the juice* never met me, or my sparring partner Amanda Finch. Amanda, with her hair forever pulled back in neat cornrows and her limbs so long and strong that if you let her get a lock on you, you'd be on the mat forever, being squeezed to a pulp. Sweetness never even comes into the picture. I'm having serious doubts about my own levels.

"I don't know about you, but she's sweet," said Ricky, her sometimes gym boyfriend, when I shared my thoughts on the matter with him. "But only if you hit that spot, if you know what I mean."

I don't, so I ask Noor, my other training buddy. We're in the locker room and she's fussing with one of those new-fangled sports hijabs that never comes undone; when she puts it on her eyes turn into dark pools so gorgeous that every now and then you'll get trapped in them, and that's when she'll unleash a combo on your ass that will leave you vowing to never look in her eyes again. But you won't be able to help it.

"How the hell should I know?" Noor says, but she also spent an hour in her fiancé's BMW last week after class, so you'd think she'd be a little wiser than me. "Engagement doesn't mean marriage, Trish. What do you think I am?"

Who does she think she's fooling? Those windows steamed themselves up? Yeah right, girl.

I am as dark as Amanda, but Indian, so it's a bit different. Amanda is from Jamaica and I'm from Trinidad but Indian Trinis are as good as black even though we're not, according to the Desis I play cards with during lunch at school (sometimes dominoes when somebody is feeling dangerous). The lunchtime Desis are actually from India and can spot pretenders immediately, the people who are sort-of but not-really. The in-betweens like me with Indian blood but without any of the culture steeped into me. We're lumped together in their minds, Amanda and me. They show me pictures of saris that they wear to Indian weddings and sometimes speak in Desi-slang around me, so I won't feel like a complete outsider, but I know I am. I'm only Indian to those who don't know the difference.

Maybe this would all matter if I didn't have the gym, but I do, so who cares?

When I get back home, I'm still thinking about all this plus my skin. Especially since Ma laid the dress on my bed for me to look at some more, I guess. Pammy's son, Christopher, is also on the bed. I like to call him Columbus because of his desire to "discover" every girl he sees who puts the brown in brown sugar. He hates the name but knows it's true. Plus, him and Pammy are the only white people on this block of co-op townhouses, so he's surrounded by people who know what good curry tastes like. Noor's theory is that all the spice in the air has infected his brain.

"You're not that dark," he says, when I tell him about Ma's comment at the mall. I don't want to ask about the juice thing because he'll probably say something disgusting and

I'll have to throw him out of my room. Besides, I'm pretty sure my juice isn't *that* sweet on account of all the fighting I do. Not MMA, because I don't like Brazilian Jiu-Jitsu and never want to be face down in anyone's crotch or trapped under a stank armpit. You want to roll around on the ground? Fine, go ahead. I'm gonna stay on my feet, thanks. So Muay Thai is where it's at for me.

Punches like a boxer.

Sharp elbows and powerful knees.

Teeps with all the force I can muster behind my right leg, a push kick that can knock you on your ass.

Swing kicks that'll sweep your legs from under you.

"Yeah?" I say, moving the dress aside and sprawling out beside him. "You're the palest guy I ever met. What would you know about it?"

Columbus punches me in the shoulder, but not that hard, even though he knows I can take it. He's not offended. Neither of us have been offended by each other since we were eight years old, when we were walking home one day from school and brushed arms. He shot away from me like a bullet and called me a dirty Paki, which upset us both. Me for obvious reasons and him because it just came out and he knew it was a bad thing to say. I forgave him after a week of sullen silences but neither of us ever forgot that I could have made it much worse for him. I could have told one of our teachers at school or (worse) Pammy, who does not tolerate that kind of shit from anybody.

Ma walks into my room and looks at us on my bed. Sees something between us that isn't there. With that look we spring apart, even though it's nothing because it's Columbus and he's a dork, a gamer, an animé nerd, which is the nerdiest kind. I've crushed on other guys, but never Columbus.

Even though he was my first kiss and, pathetically, my last.

It happened a couple years ago after we snuck some of Pammy's wine from one of the ginormous boxes she drinks it out of. I shudder to even think about it. Though the kiss itself was nice, if a little dry on account of the alcohol dehydration. But it was Columbus, of all people. I mean . . . his pipe cleaner arms couldn't hold a pencil longer than a minute at a time, whereas I can do fifty push-ups without breaking a sweat. Easy as breathing. I could break him with a flick of my wrist.

When Columbus goes home, I stop outside of Ma's bedroom door and peek inside. Ma and Dad are both in there. Normally, I stay away from her room when Dad is around, but I want to ask if we can get the dress in another color maybe. Looking through the gap between the door and the frame, I see Ma pulling on her nightgown, her skin dewy from the bath. A slip of satin flutters down over the purple bruise on her hip. Dad reaches for her and she goes into his arms.

I step away, avoiding the major creaks of the floorboards, wishing he would go back to Trinidad. He doesn't come up that often, but when he's here I can't wait for him to leave again. Back in my room I pull the covers over my head and try not to think about how early it's starting this time. The bruises, I mean. I bury my head, my rage, my fear. My hatred.

I hate him so much I could kill him.

four

I'm usually at the gym more when Dad is around. Ma thinks my Muay Thai obsession is insane but realizes that at least one of us should learn self-defense. Keeps me out of trouble and all that. She knows I train, but she doesn't know I fight. She thinks it's for exercise and protection. Sometimes I think about telling her, but I don't want to make her feel bad that I can fight.

I can fight and she won't.

Me, Amanda and Noor are the main girls that train here, though others cycle through. They get with the good-looking guys, do some kick-boxing-lite and push-ups from their knees. Other stuff on their knees, too, while the real fighters spar nightly until we almost pass out. Some of them flash big smiles at everyone and we know those are the girlfriends that are gonna end up as ring girls, and there's no fate worse than being a ring girl in a sport that actually includes girls as competitors. But sure, be eye candy.

"What's with you?" asks Amanda. Noor has gone home with The Fiancé and there's only a handful of the fighters left, trying to get in that last bit of training for the night, trying to beat some sense into themselves or the other guy. Amanda gets behind my heavy bag and holds it for my push kicks. She bends her legs, takes the force on her flexed thigh rather than her belly.

"Nothing."

She gives me a knowing look. Even though we're the same age, she's always looking at me like that. I'm beyond being offended by it, though, because it's Amanda, and she's almost a legend in our gym. She made the Canadian team last year, but a knee injury kept her from competing internationally. Still, everyone was jealous because she came off her injury even better than she was before, and how does that happen? There's no chance of her not making the team again this year.

"Your dad's back?" she asks now, out of nowhere.

How did she know?

"Don't really want to talk about it." The impact of my next kick sends her a step back.

"You train harder when he's here. Might be a good thing since you can't quit losing in the ring."

My face burns. I'm so embarrassed I can't look at her. My next few kicks are off, too. Like, I know I'm shit in the ring, but I can't help it, and I can't stop from going in there either. "You might as well quit before you get any worse," she smirks. "Come on, I'll take the train with you."

Where we're from, legends take the train, too.

Before I go, I look over at Kru, who's doing his own drills on the speed bag. He doesn't break rhythm but gives us a little nod of the head to say goodbye.

Sometimes I try to tell how old Kru is, but this is almost impossible because of his amazing skin. He could be anywhere between twenty-five and forty-five and you wouldn't be surprised at either end. Once, between rounds on a pad session, I asked him why he liked Muay Thai so much, being from the Philippines. He just sighed and gave me more push-ups to do. Kru doesn't have time to explain personal shit to people, so unless you have a question about technique, you're out of luck. Sometimes, though, he'll bring pizza to the gym when we're trying to cut weight the hardest, just to remind us what's important in life. Cheese and happiness. So we don't take ourselves too seriously.

I think I've loved Kru for years, but not like you're thinking. I don't want him to touch me or anything, you perv. I just want to spend most of my waking hours at his gym . . . but everyone has to go home sometime.

Right?

It's not parka weather yet, so we're in our standard sweats as we wait for the train together. Amanda's wearing her Team Canada gear. I wonder if the situation was reversed whether I'd hold my success over her head. She's got three belts to her name already and a social media following the rest of us could only dream of. If—in some kind of multiverse where there are an infinite number of mes standing here while the Toronto chill sneaks past the fabric of my clothes and pricks at my skin—if one of them is a champ and one of her isn't, would that make me feel sorry for her?

I sneak a glance at her. Her eyes are on the tracks. Figures. Champs and almost-champs, they're always looking ahead. So now I'm doing it, too, and feeling proud of my new focus on the immediate future. We stand there, not just waiting for the train but willing it closer. She doesn't ask me any more about my dad, and it's a blessed relief. The thing about the gym is nobody is all that interested in what your life is like outside its walls. It's just not that important.

The next few days are brutal. I stand just outside the front door and listen before I walk in on anything. Ma is shouting less than she usually does. I wonder if he's gone and done it this time, made her into the woman he's always wanted her to be. That she sometimes tries to be when she gets that look in her eye with him. All soft and sweet, like one of those prim ladies from movies about the fifties who always have the house kept well, dinner ready, and still manage to stay out of everyone's way. These days she actually tries to avoid him, step around him when he's there, turn away when she sees him coming. Maybe she's learning some

defense of her own, but I think it just makes him angrier.
I don't mean to sound judgy . . . it's just that her footwork
needs some fine-tuning.

Jab, cross, hook, uppercut. One, two, three, four. Bap bap
bap bap. It's about the rhythm, see?

"Come on," says Ricky, who's holding pads for me. "Ten
swing kicks." So I give him ten, and we go back to combos.

Knee. Double knee. Push back, swing kick. Do it fifty
times, then join conditioning class for some weight training.

I beg Kru to put me on for a demo coming up.

"You sure you're ready this time?"

"I'm ready, Kru. I want this."

He sighs. Rubs at the imaginary hairs on his jaw. "I'll
think about it."

That night, Kru's ex from last year comes in like it's nothing and watches us train from the bench. Nobody can focus
because we wonder what he's gonna do about it. She won't
leave, just sits there painting her nails. *In a Muay Thai gym.* A
drip of electric-blue polish falls on the mat and we hope he's
gonna throw down. But he doesn't. He's too busy helping us
be the best fighters we can be to even notice that basic shit.

This only makes us respect him more. Train harder, even
though it's almost impossible to ignore the presence of this

soft woman with her hard face. We want to be the best for Kru. To be ready to drop and give him fifty push-ups at any point in our day. Train harder. Be stronger. Faster. Control our emotions as he does—ignoring the ladies in our lives that make everything difficult.

Be ready for whatever life throws at us.

"You never know what can happen," Aunty K said recently. She was talking about last year in Trinidad when someone tried to kidnap my dad, which happens to people there all the time, on account of all the drugs and general mayhem. We'd even knocked Colombia off the list for most kidnappings for a while. Congrats to everybody.

Dad had the sense to defend himself and chase his attacker off, but sometimes I wish he wasn't so very prepared for what life threw at him. I see the transformation in Ma when he's around. She becomes smaller and fiercer. She cleaves onto me so tight. At these times, I know there's a difference between smothering and mothering, but I can't remember what it is.

I have this fantasy, right. Ma will come to see me fight and Kru will be there and they'll fall in love and I'll get a free gym membership forever, with a set of hand wraps thrown in.

This is some childish bullshit, I know. But I can't help it. When I heard Dad almost got taken, that's what I came back to first. Ma and me, Kru and the gym. Just us. No one else. Dad like a faded photo from the past, shoved into some dark corner where he'll never bother us again. Like somebody we used to know. Memories fading with the bruises on her body.

five

My next fight, a demo fundraiser for the gym's competition season, the one I specifically begged Kru to put me in, is a disappointment. The girl I'm up against doesn't even show, so I've got to spar in the ring with Jason, a Mexican guy a year older than me. A college boy. He trained at another gym in the city before coming here to take advantage of a week free pass, and then never left. We're the same height and he thinks he's the shit but his conditioning is lacking at best. Even though he has abs of steel, apparently they're just for show. He gets gassed in the first round and I just play him until I land a push kick to his stomach. He goes flying across the ring and Kru steps in with a giddy smile and throws both mine and Jason's hands up in victory, even though everyone knows I won.

Jason wraps me in celebratory hug. He's way too happy for a guy who just lost to a girl. I notice for the first time that he smells better than he should for a guy who just finished a fight. And I suddenly wonder how I must smell to him, which is not what I want to be thinking about after my victory.

Thankfully, the crowd is still cheering. I can tell that I made Kru proud.

Kru, with his shinbone like a blade that can slice right through you. Like one of those knives you order off the television, sharp and precise. Truly, I've never seen anything like it. Kru could have been a fighter in his own right, a contender, but he had woman troubles. That's what some people whisper behind his back. Me and the other fighters couldn't care less about that. The others tend to glare at those people until they shut up, but I mostly just ignore them. Who am I to listen to them, to judge Kru? I've got nuff woman troubles of my own.

Kru holds the ropes apart for me so I can slide through. Jason's already out, so Kru follows me with a hand on my shoulder. He's beaming and looks so happy that I start to feel happy, too. Maybe he'll even let me fight next month against that girl from that west-side gym, the one I lost to last year.

Because I'm no Jason. I can handle a hit.

The first time I took a kick to the stomach, full on with my belly relaxed, I thought I was going to die. Noor was the one that did it. It was a teep and the full force of her blow went ramming through me, an anvil of female power like you never knew existed. I dry-heaved over the bin for a good five minutes and she sat with me afterwards, her arm slung around my shoulders, while tears of frustration and pain streamed down my face.

Kru waited for me outside the ladies' locker room and raised his slim self, corded with lean muscle, to his full height while he peered at me. He's no more than an inch or so taller than me, so he can't exactly do the looking down thing he sometimes tries to do. The looking down is implied. "You have to tense, Trish," he said, rapping his hard belly.

By then I was all cried out. Only fourteen then, a baby. So soft. Pathetic. I nodded and we worked on it for the rest of the year.

Crunch. Medicine ball dropped on my stomach on the flex.

Crunch. Drop. Throw up. Crunch. Drop.

But I learned. In the end, I learned that it could feel so good.

Was this what Ma felt when my father hit her where nobody would see? A flare of pleasure in the pain?

"You let her hurt you too much," Kru had said after my first fight, which was just after I turned sixteen. It was against a Brazilian chick from Buffalo I had at least five pounds on. I should have crushed her because her right crosses were like feather taps, but she knew how to land her swing kicks, right at the spot where my quads ended and a world of pain began. I lost, by decision. Kru thought I was too hurt to fight back, a girl that small. But he was wrong, wasn't he? Because, for some reason, I found myself leaning into her blows.

After the demo I go straight home to study. I'm trying for advanced acceptance to Ryerson University for business management, and I need to have at least a B average. My grades are usually around there, but you never know. And I have to get in. Ever since Kru opened up a new gym in downtown Toronto, I don't even want to consider the other options.

I don't expect anyone to be home because Dad is usually out with his friends at all hours of the day and Ma's working day shift at the hospital, so she isn't going to be around for sure. When she's not there, there's no food, and he's not going to stick around on an empty belly.

But there he is. On the couch, watching a cricket match on TV. Eating the tamarind balls he brought for me. His phone lights up and plays an old calypso, "Bassman," but he doesn't bother to answer the call.

"What?" he says to me, when I stare at him. Or, specifically, the tamarind candy in his hand. "You wasn't eating them, Missy."

Because he's here and he's hungry I can tell he's waiting for Ma. It's in the darkness of his mood. The fact that his rum shop friends are trying to reach him but he doesn't want to answer them. So I go to the kitchen and fry up some bake, triangles of fluffy dough that I slather with butter and cheese, just the way he likes it. He doesn't even say thanks, as usual.

"You're too skinny, girl," he says, without even looking at me. "You should eat something."

"Okay."

This is a standard example of our sparkling conversation.

"You have a boyfriend yet?"

I think about Jason. "No."

"What about that boy from next door you always with?"

Columbus? Ew. "Definitely not."

Dad seems as glad about this as I am. "Good. You need to focus on your studies. Where's your Mommy?"

I hate it when he calls her my Mommy. It's a Trini thing, but still. There's no reason to keep everything from the old country. Isn't that why we came to this new country? To leave behind all the awkward crap? "At work, probably."

"Probably?"

I shrug. I'm not her keeper. Dad's phone rings just then, so I'm spared more of this quality bonding time.

"Eat something," he says before answering the phone and shouting to one of his friends about how cold it is up here. Surprise surprise. You're in Canada now. Maybe put on a jacket?

There is no way in hell I can eat fried dough post-workout, so I mix a protein shake and gulp it on the way upstairs. About an hour later I hear him leave the house. I go to the kitchen and eat the rest of the tamarind balls.

My phone buzzes. It's Columbus. *Can I come over now?* No doubt smelling the fried dough from his house. We do share a wall, after all.

Use your keys, I'm not coming down.

Not sure why Ma first gave Pammy keys, only that her and Columbus have had them hanging in their kitchen for as long as I can remember. Columbus uses them most often to scrounge around for food, but not usually when Dad is here. I guess we've both been waiting for Dad to leave, for the reprieve. I hope there's some to spare for Ma.

six

Maybe the fumes from the bake and cheese went to his head, or it could be that I finally did something right, because Dad comes to pick me up from the gym the next day for some extra quality bonding time.

I'm sparring when I see him watching from the doorway.

He looks . . . proud? I mean, I'm doing pretty well if I do say so myself, so why wouldn't he be? I guess it's just a new feeling, is all, and it's super freaking weird to see him there. He usually has other things to do, like . . . okay, I can't really think of what else he does when he comes up from Trinidad. Whatever it is, it's not picking me up from anything. Dad's a big believer in using Ma's car while other people take public transit.

"How's your Mommy been?" he asks, as we walk to the parking lot.

"Good." I can feel the sweat cooling on my body, turning sticky. I don't mind taking the train in this stench, but I am glad for the ride. Even though I'd never say it to him.

"She working a lot?"

I shrug. "I guess." Ma always works a lot, though. So it's not been much different.

"She going out and seeing she friends on the weekend?"

What's with the interest in Ma's whereabouts and weekend activities all of a sudden? "I don't know. I've been busy with school," I say, because I'm not going to snitch on anybody. Even if Ma was missing for months, I still wouldn't tell him.

It doesn't look like he believes me but suddenly he grins and puts a hand on my shoulder like we're old pals. The thing about my dad is that when he smiles it really suits him. You're not supposed to tell people they should smile more because they look better when they do, but with him it's actually true. I can almost see what Ma sees in him when he's like this.

Almost but not quite.

On the drive home, he asks some questions about school and I tell him about my plans to be in business management. He likes the sound of that a lot but flat out tells me I should get a part-time job to supplement my student loans for college because he's saving for his retirement.

I nod and say that's a great idea but obviously it isn't. How can I train, go to school *and* work? This is why I lost my job at Foot Locker. It's like the man doesn't even know me.

I should ask Kru if there are any tourneys with cash prizes. Maybe when I turn pro.

For the next several days I just try to live my best life before I have to get a job to pay for college, on top of everything else. I tell Ma about the conversation in the car.

"He picked you up from the gym?" she asks again. She's frowning. I guess we're both shook by that. "Why did he want to know about how I spend my weekends? Don't I deserve a break, too?"

She's completely missing the point about how getting a job would interfere with my training. I try to explain it to her, but she waves it away. "Tell me again exactly what he asked about me. His exact words, Trisha."

Does she think I don't know what exactly means? But I know better than to say that out loud. As I start to recap the whole boring event yet again, she gets a look in her eye that I don't understand. One that I don't particularly like. I guess I should be paying better attention.

Toward the end of Dad's latest stay with us, Aunty K comes to spend the weekend, all spontaneous-like.

Aunty K lives in New York and often spends her holidays with us because she's alone, never been married or had kids, and has no other options.

So she's our burden, I guess?

Ma forces me to go to dinner the evening Aunty K arrives, even though she knows I'm trying to cut weight.

"Ma, do I have to go?" I ask. I got a few rounds of sparring in earlier and I'm sore as hell. But also hungry. "Can you bring me some takeout?"

"Get in the car, Trisha," she snaps.

You know, there's no talking to her when she's like this.

I do get in the car, in my elastic-waist sweats because we're going for Chinese food and I already know how this night is going to end. With me bloated and regretful.

But I'm wrong.

I mean, not really. I do end up bloated and regretful, but that's not all.

It ends up being the craziest night of my life.

seven

We're in the car on our way back home. Outside of the restaurant, Ma said I should drive and got in the passenger seat before I could ask if she was sure. It's raining, one of those fall showers that started in the afternoon and goes into the night. Ever since I got my learner's permit, Ma has let me drive as much as possible, but it's weird for me to drive in this wet darkness. Maybe she thinks I need the experience.

We don't speak.

It feels like we're waiting for something, even as we coast down our street, into the co-op townhouse complex, and pull into the parking lot.

That something is at home. We can feel it, sense it. Drawing closer.

I don't want us to go home yet but Ma is tired. I can see it in the circles under her eyes, the set of her jaw. There's something else, some other look that I might have put there. Nothing I seem to do tonight is right. Ma's on edge and has been snapping at me more than usual. Aunty K starts to chatter to cut the tension, but this is just for her own benefit.

Maybe the rain is why it happens the way it does. A screech of tires and a dull thud against the front bumper. A scream coming from somewhere. It hurts my ears, rings through my head, blurs my vision . . .

"Stop," my mother whispers. Aunty K is silent now, for once.

The scream dies out in my throat.

It seems like forever before Ma gets out of the car to see what we hit. Rather, who. She's trembling. Kneeling beside Dad. Checking to see if he's alive.

He's not.

Before the police come to the crime scene, Ma leaves Aunty K for a moment while she takes me aside. I can't speak. Now the screaming is done, I have nothing left. She gets real close and we're now eye to eye. "Listen carefully," she says. And then she tells me what the story is.

"That's what happened, okay?" she says, when she's done.

Why is she so calm? "Okay."

"Remember: you were driving."

I nod. It's true. "I was driving."

"And you didn't see him."

I look away from her. It happened so fast. I don't know what I saw. I don't know what anyone saw.

We don't have any more time to talk because that's when the police get there. Because I'm shook and I'm babbling and Ma's right beside me listening to every word I say, this is what I tell the cop: I don't even think about Dad when he's around. A long time ago I learned to pretend he wasn't even there. I have a dad, yeah, but he could be anywhere in the world. Most likely back in Trinidad, at his house he shares with another woman.

Where in Trinidad?

Um, a place called Diego Martin.

And what did he do there?

He could be doing anything, but he's definitely not doing anything with me.

It sounds bad, that part, so I adjust and say that he owns a garage and he works there, too. Fixing cars. Though I have never in my whole life seen him fix a damn thing. Or get anything, or do anything for himself. He just looked at me and said Missy, pass me this or Missy, go and do that. Missy, am I talking to you? Missy, don't you have something else to do?

Missy, hey you. Never Trisha, my name.

I try to listen to the cop, but it's hard because Ma is paying real close attention to what I'm saying, and also to the things that I'm not.

The cop asks some questions, but I start to feel real queasy. Worse than when Noor landed her teep and I threw up over the garbage bin.

"You were driving, right?"

I nod.

"How fast were you going?"

"I don't remember. I just turned the corner into the parking lot, so probably not fast." Dinner isn't sitting well and I'm so nauseous after what happened that I throw up on his shoes.

That ends the interview quick.

The cop already talked to Ma and Pammy. I heard Pammy tell him that she'd seen the whole thing from her window. Now he moves on to Aunty K, who manages to keep all her greasy Chinese food down while he asks her questions about tonight. Questions about Dad.

Apparently Dad had a split lip that didn't look like it happened during the accident. Aunty K says she doesn't know anything about that.

He asks why she showed up inexplicably to take me and Ma to dinner. All the way from New York, closing up her roti shop for a few days. She tells him that she just wanted to spend some time with Ma and me. She doesn't tell him that Dad didn't come with us because he was never able to look her in the eye, on account of his messed-up relationship with Ma. Maybe that's why he went out with his friends tonight. Could also be why he was sneaking around in the parking lot in the rain. He didn't want us to notice him. If so, he did a pretty bad job of staying out of the way. All things considered.

The cop thinks so, too. That he wasn't good at dodging, especially tonight.

What a tragic accident.

eight

Thank God for Columbus. His constant presence in our house can be a pain sometimes but after the accident, I actually appreciate it.

Two days after Dad dies, I come into the kitchen and no one's around but him. He's making a grilled cheese sandwich, and even offers me some of it. He breaks it in two and hands me the smaller piece. "You need to fix the back door. It's broken or something."

"You didn't use your key?" He normally comes in through the front door like he owns the place.

He finishes his half of the sandwich in seconds, still standing, and rummages through the fridge for more food. "My mom has it in her purse and I don't know where she went. Kind of dangerous to have a broken back door in this neighborhood, Trish. I put our door blocks in there for you guys, but you should get a new lock."

Like I don't know that. "I'll deal with it," I say.

But actually, I forget all about it, because it turns out that Ma wants me out of the house almost immediately. Apparently, my studies are the most important thing right now. She says. And she must be right, since she's been watching me real close ever since Dad died.

So I'm back at school and everyone who knows about the accident treats me like I have the plague. The lunchtime Desis don't know how to talk to me, so we just play cards and pretend that nobody died. While we sit there eating our PB&J, they silently imply the loss of a father should be a bigger deal. I should be weeping and pulling my hair out like I'm in a Bollywood film or something. But I can't be bothered because I have training to do and a mother to wonder about.

I can't stand their pitying looks during our lunchtime card games. Like I'm the broken one. Me. Not Dad.

The only person who acknowledges something is up to my face is the school's only guidance counselor, Mrs. Nunez, but she's too day drunk (as usual) to care that much. I sit in her office, which is full of psychology books I bet she's never read. She takes her sweet time to go over my file, to remember who I am and why I've been sitting in her office for the past five minutes. When she reaches the part in my file where it says my dad just died, she puts on an appropriately concerned expression. I spend about ten minutes saying I'm sad. Yes, it was a tragedy. Horrible. Some other adjectives thrown in. Once, an adverb. She asks if I need help. I say no, because of the warning glances Ma has been shooting me at home.

Omertà, Ma. I get it. My lips are firmly sealed around my mouth guard.

My English teacher hands me a book after class on my first day back. He's been giving me sad looks ever since he heard about Dad.

"What's this, Mr. Abdi?" I say, even though I can see it's clearly a novel.

"*Soucouyant*, by David Chariandy. A local Trinidadian author. I thought you might want to do your final essay on this. It's from your culture."

Okay, hold up. This diversity thing has gotten out of hand. I don't need to be racially profiled like this! Why can't I have *The Great Gatsby* like everyone else? But I don't say that, obviously. I say thanks and slip the slim volume into my bag. I've heard about soucouyants but I don't know why anybody would want to write a book about some unknown vampires from the Caribbean.

"I hope you take some English classes when you go to college. I think you have something, Trisha." Then he looks embarrassed, like he shouldn't have said this at all.

I smile at him like I'm gonna think about it, but what's the point? I'm on my way to a degree in business manage-ment, no matter what he thinks. All this "books improve lives" BS he doles out from time to time falls deaf on our cash-strapped immigrant ears. We all know what's up. Get good jobs, marry richer or up the color-line, buy houses, take care of our overworked parents who keep reminding us that they put us into the world and they can take us out of it at any time. We don't have time for this literature shit. How are we supposed to pay off student loans with an English degree?

There's no training today.

Kru is teaching at the downtown gym and I don't want to take two buses and a train all the way over there in hopes of a short pad session, so I decide to skip it. Plus, I've got at least three hours of homework ahead of me.

I walk home from the bus stop and see Pammy watching me from her window. It's cold, the moment before winter clenches the whole city in its grip. As I take my gloved hands out of my jacket to fish around for my keys, I can feel her intensity. Pammy sends me these looks sometimes, like, *I'm so sorry, boo, that your Ma still has a man in her life.* Because Pammy sent her ex packing three years ago after what Columbus calls the Worst Fucking Day of His Whole Fucking Life.

It started at Canada's Wonderland, an amusement park they had to drive for what seemed like hours just to get to. The whole thing was set off by Columbus back-talking his father in one way or another. Maybe he didn't say anything at all—Columbus doesn't always remember it the same way—maybe it was just a look. But what he doesn't forget is when his dad went off the rails and whaled on him like you wouldn't believe, right in front of everybody. He'd just lost his construction job and was maybe looking for some energy to expend, or maybe he hated Columbus just as much as we all suspected—whatever the reason, Pammy wasn't having it.

She booted him out, pressed charges, bought herself a box of wine and a giant-ass container of bubble bath, and deliriously soaked him away. Columbus said she read *Wild* and *Eat Pray Love* back-to-back in the cramped, standard-issue co-op tub that we've all tried to fold ourselves into, and that was it.

Blonde Lady Epiphany.

After a few days, she changed the locks and started acting like a lesbian, according to Columbus. She even cut her hair and everything. I saw her on a date once, at a sushi restaurant near my gym. Her short hair was spiked up with gel and looked as if it could cut you if you came too close. She had her hand on a be-dreaded man's arm and he was smiling like all his birthdays had come at once. I don't know what happened with the man. I never saw him again and never mentioned it to Columbus, because she seemed to not be fully committed to the whole lesbian thing. Plus, guys can't handle truths about their mothers, no matter how woke they seem. I mean, I can barely manage it with my own. And that was before I started reading the soucouyant book.

After, it was impossible to look her in the eye.

Soucouyants are like this: During the day, they're fusty old ladies who somehow smell both like feet and lemon disinfectant. At night, they shed their old-lady skin and turn into balls of fire that go flying about in the sky and slip under people's doorways and then, I dunno, become vampires that suck the blood right out of you.

Ridiculous, right?

Except.

Except I heard this lady talking in Aunty K's roti shop once and she swore the soucouyant who was biting her father-in-law was the hot chick from the next village over. Her friend agreed that this was possible, you done know, and they got another round of peanut punch to last them through a discussion of how, in some of these stories, the soucouyants are beautiful young women. They're fluid like that.

Young, beautiful, old, hideous . . . it doesn't matter.

The monster is female and she comes for you at night.

The thing about the soucouyant book is that it gave me nothing but the knowledge that monsters live in our heads. Which I already knew, yeah? I skimmed through the rest of the novel looking for . . . what? Advice? Clues?

But it wasn't what I needed. It scared me because there's

so much about monsters that we don't know, that we can never understand.

I would have ignored the book and the roti shop talk, except the funeral happens that same week and everything changes. I see that look Ma shares with Pammy and Aunty K. I remember Ma's face when she asked why Dad wanted to know about her comings and goings. I remember being in the car the night Dad died, and I start to wonder about Ma.

present day

THE MASTER PLAN:

Get degree in Business Management
Work at a bank
Start saving for retirement
Marry a banker
Use some retirement savings for a mortgage
Pay mortgage for the rest of our lives
Die

IN THE MEANTIME:

Don't talk about the accident
Work on Muay Thai technique
Win next fight
Win fight after that
Keep my mouth shut
Win more fights
Maybe die

nine

A week after the funeral I turn in my essay on *The Great Gatsby*, like everybody else. Mr. Abdi can't hide his disappointment. His hangdog mouth hangs even further and he looks at me with those big blue eyes that look so out of place in his dark face. I mean, geez. What's with the guilt fest? It's just an essay.

I hand him back the soucouyant book.

"You didn't like it?" he asks, trying hard to sound all casual. Failing, because it's hard to fake casual when you're almost in tears over an essay. "You could have written about that, how it didn't resonate."

"I didn't finish it," I say.

This, I think, is even worse. If I let my feelings show on my face like Mr. Abdi does, I'd be even more shit in the ring than I already am.

"I see. I'd hoped it would spark something . . . well, don't let this discourage you, Trisha. You write well and I know you enjoy the assigned readings, so I hope you consider pursuing your love for literature in the future. Even as a reader. We need more of those in the world." He gives me a sad kind of smile and busies himself with the papers on his desk.

I get the feeling I'm not the first immigrant kid he's tried to beat over the head with a book on their "culture" and, knowing what little I do know of him, I'm probably not going to be the last. Everybody has dreams, even bizarre ones, like Mr. Abdi's.

When I leave, I try not to look back at him or the book that ruined my life and put ideas in my head. Teaching me about the evil that comes from my homeland. I try not to think of Dad. I used to think he was evil on account of him and Ma but now I don't really know what evil is. Anyway, the book is out of my hands now.

Sayonara, Advanced English.

Business Management, here I come.

But his reaction to my essay bothers me all the way to the gym because Mr. Abdi is one of the decent ones. He actually cares. Once, he'd noticed a bruise on my arm and notified Mrs. Nunez. She obviously *didn't* care and was visibly relieved when I explained it happened during training and, yes, I'm a fighter and, yes, my mother knows all about it. But at least he noticed. More than anyone else.

I forget all about the conversation at sparring because the gym is packed and sweat is pouring off us. Nobody can think of anything but getting a good few rounds in. Kru is in a good mood today, so we're working on spinning elbows and Superman punches—the flying ones. This is the flashy stuff that you don't pull out in fights. You only do these if you get hired to do stunts on a movie set or something. Can't spin my elbow for shit, but I get some nice height on my Superman.

Soon we're dizzy and airborne.

It's all going to our head. Jason, the guy I beat at the demo, is terrible at Supermans—

Supermen?

—but I think he's having the best time out of us all. I'm even smiling, which I haven't done since the night Dad died. I'm smiling so much I see other people doing it, too, and it doesn't go away, this feeling, until I get home.

My gear is so disgusting that I throw it all in the washing machine as soon as I walk in the door. There, next to the washer, I look at the sliding back door. Right. A couple days after Dad died, Columbus told me it was broken. The door blocks he put there are still in place, though. I think they work just fine to keep anyone from getting in, but we should probably fix it.

"Ma?" I say, coming up the stairs. "We need a new latch for the back door."

"What?" she calls from the kitchen. Her hair is piled high on her head and she's zoning out at the kitchen table, looking like she's not even in the same world.

"The back door. A couple days after Dad died Columbus told me it was broken but I forgot to tell you. Sorry.

Columbus put in door blocks but we probably need a new lock."

She blinks at me until what I'm saying registers, even though it's a pretty basic thing. Broken. Back door. New lock. Not complicated.

But a whole heap of emotions flit across her face. Maybe it was the easy way I brought up Dad's death. I should have found a different way to put it. "Did you see the door blocks Columbus put in, Ma?"

"No, Trisha. What a question. If I knew, I would have known the door was broken and asked you to help me fix it," she says, yawning. "Go to the hardware store tomorrow after school, get a new lock and we'll put it in."

"I wonder how long it's been like that, though. I haven't been in the basement since the last time I washed my gear, which was the day before Dad died. And the lock definitely worked then."

"Is that so?"

"So it must have broken sometime between just before he died and when Columbus saw it a couple days later."

"Alright, Nancy Drew, will you please stop with this? I just asked you to get a new lock, okay?"

I flinch. I mean, all I'm trying to do is make a point. "Okay. Can I have some money for the lock?"

She passes over her purse and doesn't even seem to notice how much I'm taking. So I pocket a little extra, because I'm strapped. And I'm gonna pay it back eventually. It's not like she doesn't know where I live.

She goes to bed with a glass of water and two extra-strength painkillers and I do my homework in the living room.

I go downstairs to do some laundry. And that brings me back to what happened with the lock on our back door. If I didn't break it, and Ma sure seemed to be oblivious, who did? It's not like it broke itself.

Did someone try to break in here or something?

I can't think about this now. Ma doesn't want me to and none of it makes sense, anyway.

After homework and laundry, I watch playback of my first fight with the Brazilian girl from Buffalo. I'm trying to learn from my mistakes but all I can see is how much damage she inflicts. She's a lighter shade of brown than me and moves so fast when she's of a mind to do it that she's just a beige streak of motion. But I'm stronger. You could see it from the jump. I could have stopped her at any point. She's fast, but I'm letting her catch me. In the video I look tired, but not as tired as I feel these days.

Why am I so run down all the time now?

I bet I just need to be faster. Yeah, that's it exactly.

"Kru," I say, the next day. "I need some speed training." I came to the gym right after school, almost bursting with this insight. I couldn't sit still in economics and narrowly avoided being handed detention for trying to get away early, but important things like speed training can't wait.

He looks at me for a moment and then takes me into his back office where we set up a schedule. Amanda sticks her head in to say something and he motions her inside. "I'm starting you girls on speed training, all of you."

I can't keep the disappointment off my face. Amanda can't stop grinning, the bitch. Soon Noor will get in on this and I'll have to share him with someone else.

But Noor is the least of my problems because two days later Imelda Isaacs shows up and things get from bad to worse.

Some people might not like to hear this, but it's a common myth in Scarborough, the east end of Toronto, where I live, that white girls are easier than every other kind of girl around—and there are lots of different kinds of girls, because it's Scarborough and you can't throw a stone without hitting someone from a country you've never even heard of before. Even though it's not true (I've personally seen plenty of skanks of both the male and female variety in every color of the rainbow), the myth exists. I mean, I thought everyone knew about it, but apparently nobody ever told Imelda Isaacs, the new girl at the gym. Imelda's a ginger so pale that her eyelashes are invisible. All you see of her eyes are wide open blue. She has a kind of Noor effect because everyone who spars with her has to stop themselves from drowning in them.

Everyone around her is spun, even me, and I can't hate her even though I want to because she's so much better than me.

"How did you get so good?" I ask her.

"Oh, I used to do Brazilian Jiu-Jitsu, so I'm used to really intense training," she says, and she's smiling for no reason at all because that's the kind of person she is and we're all finding it impossible to hate on her for it.

Now everyone wants some BJJ classes at the gym and everyone is asking Imelda for tips on how to improve their ground game. Kru is a staunch Muay Thai guy, but even he sees a financial opportunity when one slaps him with a speed bag. So we're doing BJJ now, recreationally, and some idiot tells Imelda the whole white chicks are easier thing and she knocks his ass straight into a wall of mirrors, which is understandable but unfortunate. The mirror cracks, sending the whole thing crashing down. Shattering into a thousand little pieces. There's glass everywhere and the whole gym is a lawsuit waiting to happen . . . I mean, if this wasn't Kru's gym. Nobody would ever sue Kru. Wouldn't even dare.

The gym is closed for a couple days while the mats are being replaced. I think Kru is mad at us, maybe the comment even got back to him, so he's punishing everyone for the idiot (who'd also said some unflattering things about the Punjabi contingent of middle-schoolers that come to train Saturday afternoons). Flags from all the countries represented at the gym hang from the ceiling and if there's anything that bothers Kru it's the kind of talk that makes anyone feel unwelcome. He doesn't stand for it. We leave personal shit at the door and only the dumbest of fucks mess with that. But now someone did and I've got nowhere to go after school.

Racism, damn. It affects everyone's training schedules, I mean, lives.

Ma has forgotten all about the back door, but I can't open my wallet without looking at all the extra money in there. After getting a new lock from the hardware store, Columbus and I watch videos online on how to install locks. We smoke some weed while we mess around with the door. Finally, we get the new lock in.

Columbus wants to smoke more, but I'm looking at my fingernails and imagining them growing longer, sharp enough to do as much damage as my razor-like teeth. There's a cut on my thigh, probably from the glass at the gym, and I can't stop staring at it.

I tell Columbus to go home.

"You have no chill," he says, rolling his eyes. But I'm plenty chill right now. That night I dream about nails that lengthen into claws, pointed and sharp, and wake up with my fingers on the cut on my thigh. There's no more sleep for me tonight, so I go downstairs and find Ma at the kitchen table.

"How was work?" I ask her.

"Same thing every day," she says. She's still in her nurse's uniform. "Did you eat?"

"Yeah."

"Still hungry? Want me to make you something?"

"No, Ma."

"You can speak in full sentences, you know." But there's a tired smile on her face when she says this. "I'm going to bed."

She hugs me when she gets up, so quick that I'm unprepared. Before I can fight her off, the hug is over and she presses a kiss to my temple. It goes straight to the hurt there, that I hadn't even remembered until this moment. She never does stuff like this and I think she must be upset over Dad so I tell myself I should watch her more. I'm not gonna ask about him—we don't talk about him now any more than we used to—but I'm gonna pay more attention.

I guess what I'm trying to say is that I'm home after school these days, watching for Ma, so I don't miss the next big imposition in my life. Maybe even bigger than Imelda Isaacs and this BJJ nonsense, because who shows up next is the man who will bust more than just a wall of glass. It will be my life. In a thousand sharp little pieces.

ten

I come home after training and voila. A whole new problem in my life in the form of a stranger inside the house with Ma. Without any kind of explanation, nothing. He's just there, eating a mushroom pizza from the freezer that I've been saving for one of my carb-overloading days. Ma isn't eating. She looks a bit tense, to be honest, as she introduces him to me. His name is Ravi. I've always hated that name. I've never met a good Ravi in my life, or even a useful one.

"Did you know my dad?" I ask Ravi. I mean, I'm so confused. Ma doesn't let people into our house easily. Sometimes I was surprised Dad got past the front door.

The look that passes between them is charged. Ravi reaches for Ma's hand and I'm so shocked that I can't even speak.

"No," he says.

I sense Ma is furious at me, for some reason, so I shut the hell up and lock myself into my bedroom for the rest of the night. They go upstairs together later, and I can't even believe it.

I hope she's washed Dad off her sheets.

I remember something from a while back.

Two months of hard training for a fight in Buffalo left me exhausted and near-starving. But cutting weight is no joke. I fight at 115 but I'm naturally 125. I heard my opponent came in at 130 when she's off weight, so I was at a disadvantage anyway, but what the hell. I had three pounds to go and I'd been running in saran wrap every day. I was nothing but muscle, sinew and bones—and a lot of hair, which I pulled ruthlessly into a braid every day, or waxed off, if it was on the wrong part of my body, if you know what I mean. (You know what I mean, right?) But I couldn't stop cutting because Amanda and Noor had already made weight with a week left and were looking fierce as fuck. They were keeping up with the guys on chin-ups, too, an ability I lose when I get too skinny. It's the light-headedness that unbalances me.

So I went downstairs after midnight for something quick to eat. I'd heard Ma in the shower earlier so I knew she was home from the hospital.

She should have been asleep in bed, but she wasn't. I ate peanut butter with a spoon, straight from the jar, and caught a glimpse of two shadows in the parking lot right outside of our corner unit, the last unit on our block. The shadows parted and a man walked to a car at the far end of the lot. That would have been the end of the story right there if he didn't pause before getting in. Paused right under the street-light so that he could get one last look at her. I could feel his smile even from a distance. I crept back up the stairs and was in bed by the time Ma came back into the house and creaked open my door to check that I was asleep. I wasn't but my back was to her so she couldn't possibly have known that.

My back turned, eyes open, mouth gummy with peanut butter and confusion. Dad wasn't up from Trinidad. Who was that man? And what was Ma doing with him so late at night?

I want to see if there's any mushroom pizza left, but I don't want to run into Ma or Ravi. So I just do homework until there's no more homework to do, then I lie in my bed and think about the soucouyant book. It's not like I can think about *Gatsby*, because what I wrote in my essay was true: it was kind of boring and about people who make no sense to me. The soucouyant book, though, it makes a lot of sense. Mr. Abdi was on to something when he gave it to me. Maybe he knew I would find some uncomfortable stuff in there, but it's not like I can actually admit that.

The thing about soucouyants is that once one of them gets her hands on you, she doesn't let go. She can bleed you for years. When you wake up there are little scratches on your body, on your neck. You feel like your life is draining away right before your eyes. Over the years you become weaker and weaker. You stop fighting. You let her take everything you have and don't say boo. She's not in it for the fast bleed; she plays the long game and lives off your life force until she's through with you and moves on to the next sucker.

When I got a look at Ravi sitting there eating my pizza like it was his all along, I saw something in him that I've only ever seen in myself.

A sucker.

How could she even get a new man so quick, you ask? Yeah, I was wondering the same thing as I stared at him in a kinda shocked haze, until I realized where I'd seen him before.

He's the guy she was with in the shadows of the parking lot.

I know it's him, know it from the salt-and-pepper of his hair, from the bend in his nose, from the smile he flashed to her under the streetlight. Illuminated for a split second, caught in the camera flash of my memory.

Snap.

There you are, new man. In our lives, outside of our house, in the months before my father died under the wheels of our car.

eleven

It's just a week away from Christmas holidays. Dad's urn is side-eyeing us from the living room and I'm sitting at the table with Ravi, who turns out to be another Trini guy, because Ma's man-barometer apparently is broken and has just one setting. He's not tall like Dad was, but he's a solid bulk in our dining room. His hair is slicked back off his forehead and I can't tell his age.

He's looking at me and I know exactly what he's thinking.

He's wondering what kind of problem I'll be.

I silently send the signal that I'm gonna be the biggest problem he could possibly imagine, but the main issue with that is that he doesn't seem to have much of an imagination.

We stare at each other like this until Ma comes in. She sets a plate of red beans and rice in front of him. I watch him eat, the beans stewed thick with tomatoes and garlic, just the way I like it best.

"You not hungry?" he asks, nodding to my full plate, which I just pick at. These are the first words he has spoken to me. Unlike most West Indian men I've met, he's not much of a talker.

"No."

There's something in my voice that makes my mother look up at me, that makes her pretty brown eyes flash a warning so dire that I have never been able to ignore it. Until now.

"Eat your food," she says.

I've never disobeyed a direct order from her before, but I've had it with the two of them. This on top of Imelda and the new BJJ at our gym? Not today, Satan.

"No." I push away from the table and am out the door before either of them can say boo. I'm quicker than they'd ever imagined. Even though we're just starting our speed training, I'm like lightning.

At the gym, which is now open again, I sit on a bench in the corner and watch Jason spar with Ricky, both on the card for a tourney in Montreal.

"What's the matter?" Jason calls from the ring, after they do their rounds. Since I beat his ass at the demo he's been paying extra attention to me but I haven't taken the bait. Who wants a guy you can drop with a single push kick? I do have to say, he looks tight these days, so at least he's learning.

"Leave her be," says Kru, passing by. He gives me a pat on the shoulder and hands me a bottle of disinfectant and roll of paper towels for the gym equipment. This is no Mr. Miyagi, wax-on-wax-off shit. This is because I haven't paid membership in months and I've got to contribute somehow. I haven't paid because I lost my job at Foot Locker after I missed a shift due to my last fight, and those uncompromising assholes wrote me out of the schedule. So no scratch for me right now.

I clean instead of training, letting the sharp smell go to my already light head.

When I get home I'm a wraith, a shadow, full of cleaning fumes and nothing else. Ravi's gone and I don't hear Ma anywhere. But then there she is, in the kitchen, coming at me from out of nowhere. She slaps me with her open hand, grabs the rolling pin off the counter and strikes me so hard across my shoulders I think my bones will be crushed.

Her voice is low and sharp.

"You be grateful for the food I cook. Be. Grateful. You don't know what I've done to bring you here from Trinidad for a better life. You don't know what they do to people over there. This is what you say? This is what you do? You can't respect your elders?"

She raises the pin again and whips it at my head. I duck, because I'm slippery like that. It hits the wall, which only makes her angrier. I stare at the dent it has made, like a right cross with all your power behind it, the ones you make sometimes with your chin untucked because you're so in the moment that you don't care about protecting your face. You know you can do damage. And there it is, cracking the sea-green paint of our kitchen, just under the cheap plastic clock that's been there forever.

She doesn't cry and neither do I. Because I *am* grateful. Even when Dad was alive, it was always just the two of us, and everything she does is for me so that I could have the kind of life she didn't when she was growing up. If I didn't have Ma, I wouldn't have anybody. She loves me the way that nobody has ever loved her. She tells me this over and over. She hits me with love and stops before I die from her blows. Even though it would be so easy to do, I don't block her because she needs this. It's what I get from sparring, if I'm honest.

You okay? Columbus texts. He must have seen me come in, heard the rolling pin crashing into the wall. I don't answer because no, genius. No, I'm not.

After Ma disappears into her room and shuts her door, I try to fall asleep. I want to sink into the silence, let it wrap around me, pull me close and down into sleep. But silence has never been my friend. Out of it, a sound can come hurtling at me, something mean and dark, a slap across a cheek, a cry of pain. Cries of other kinds, too, which I never want to hear or think about, even less than the pain-cries.

I wait in the silence, listening for some new shift in my existence. I don't want to say my heart beats faster or my belly's full of butterflies, or anything corny like that. I know better and, because of Mr. Abdi, I also know these are lazy descriptions for a feeling that I can't even put into words. I'm not scared right now or even angry. I'm tired, but I stay up just in case. On the off chance that there's gonna be something more waiting for me tonight.

twelve

The next morning is Saturday, thank God. So I won't have to be at school, pretending that every inch of my body isn't sore. And although I heard Ma leave earlier, there are sounds downstairs that I can't place. When I emerge from my bedroom in shorts and a tank top, Pammy is in our kitchen, making pancakes. "Hey, Trish. Come eat."

She holds out a chair for me, so I slink into it and stare at the pancakes. They're hot, and they're there. Once I start eating, I can't seem to stop.

"Christopher might come over for some in a bit. I hope you don't mind," she says.

I shake my head, mouth still full. Why would I mind Columbus being here? He practically lives at my house when Ma isn't around, as Pammy well knows. But she's being careful, and I get the feeling she wants to talk about last night, what she might have heard. But I don't have the patience for all that. I hurt everywhere.

"Thanks, Pammy," I say, trying to sound okay.

Not sure if she buys it, but she doesn't push. "You're welcome, hon. Your mom had to leave early, and she said I could come over and use your television. She's got a whole season of *Sherlock* recorded and I need to get some knitting done."

Something about the easiness in her voice tells me that nobody is fooling anybody. She's deliberately not looking at the dent in the wall that is shining at us like a bruise. She's here to make sure I'm fine, and that my mother is, too. Because we're a village, in this section of the co-op. I don't think she knows about the beating (I don't think she'd be okay with that), but she knows my mom will fling things about when she's good and mad. Which isn't often, but when it happens, Pammy hears it all.

Maybe it's because I'm so relaxed with all the carbs in my belly (which I'll have to work out later), but I feel like I can trust her with something that's been on my mind.

"Hey, Pammy?"

"Yeah?" She turns back to me.

"Remember that night? The night my dad died?"

Her expression shutters closed. "I do."

"I saw you talk to the police when—after it happened. You said you saw the whole thing from your window."

She knows exactly what I mean by *it*. "I was in my kitchen, making some chamomile tea, and happened to look out. I heard your car pull into the lot."

"Right. I know about that. But did you . . . did you see anyone else there that night?"

She goes still. "No. Why? Why do you ask?"

"No reason. It's just we didn't even see my dad when we drove into the lot. But you saw everything and I was wondering if there was anyone else who could have seen it."

"I didn't see anyone else. It was raining, hon." She looks at me closely. "Have you been sleeping enough? You look tired."

"But if you could see what happened from that distance, then maybe you could see him? Dad. Did you know he was there?"

"Nobody knew he was there," she says sharply. "Honestly, Trisha, I think you need to try to forget about it. I think you need to move on."

The door to our little townhouse opens and she brightens. "There's Christopher! And just in time for some pancakes, too. If you can spare a few for him, that is." Then she winks at me, which freaks me out as Pammy doesn't do things like "brighten" and wink. But I don't have time to think about it because Columbus has made it up the stairs with his slow ass and he's looking like he's gonna fall over from the effort.

I try not to look too glad to see him, but I'm grateful for a (semi) male presence somehow. I don't know what's up with the ladies in my life right now, but I'm thinking they won't be this weird always, right?

When Columbus finishes the rest of the pancakes, we go over to his house to compare notes for economics class.

"What are you doing?" he asks, when I pause in his kitchen, which is a mirror image of mine. The view, let's be honest, isn't great. We've had one major snowfall this year, but the snow melted almost as soon as it touched the ground. So it looks the same as it did a month ago. There's not much to see out that window, other than a wooded area that backs out onto a ravine. And one part of the parking lot. Their kitchen has a full, unobstructed view of the corner where we always park. Where my father died.

"Earth to Trisha," Columbus says, coming up behind me. He punches my shoulder. "What are you looking at?"

"Nothing," I say.

I open the cupboard above the electric kettle. There's a French press and a bag of coffee beans next to the grinder that Pammy uses every morning. She puts a bit of the beans in the grinder, adds that to the French press, and pours hot (but not boiling) water over the whole thing. I've seen her do it a thousand times. "Where's your chamomile tea?"

Columbus snorts. "What are we, senior citizens?"

Exactly. I close the cupboard. "Let's study."

"Wanna make out instead?" he says, grinning at me.

"Get the fuck out of here."

"I would," he laughs, "but it's my house. You're gonna miss your chance with me, you know. We're going to college in the fall and I don't know about you, but I plan to meet a hot foreign exchange student and have loads of mad sex with her and then move to Europe where I find out she's rich and we'll live off her trust fund for the rest of our wasteful lives."

"I have the same plan, so let's see who gets there first."

I fake a punch.

He flinches.

What a baby. Like any hot foreign exchange student is going to go for *that*.

I spend the night thinking about my dad. The big spaces in my life where he's never been. You would think the garage he ran in Trinidad was the Rockefeller empire or something, the way he always needed to be back there. When I was ten I spent a week with him. Ma couldn't, or wouldn't, come with us. He took me to Maracas, on that death-defying mountain drive, all twisty and terrifying. We had bake and shark on the beach and he laughed at my pineapple chutney. He was happy there on the island, happier than he'd ever been in Toronto with me and Ma. But he loved her, couldn't stay away from her. I think she loved him, too. Mostly.

The beatings didn't start right away when he'd come up, a few weeks at a time. They would have maybe two good days, and then she'd say something, do something—little, of course. It wasn't ever a big deal. But I guess he had that in common with Columbus's dad. Just a little thing to set them off and then wham.

She's on the ground and he's whaling on her.

Okay, so I hated him.

Hated him as much as I loved her. He never touched me. Never loved me enough to lay hands on me, maybe. Or maybe my mother would never let him. I think she'd die before she let anyone else beat me. That was her job alone. That, and loving me.

Because I was always hers.

Things were better when he wasn't here. It's not like I miss him or anything. Why would I? So why can't I stop thinking about him? I only stop when I'm sparring—and it's not like I can spar forever.

But I try.

In the ring now and going at Jason hard. He wants fight prep for his tourney in Montreal? I'll give him fight prep.

"Whoa," he says, wheezing. Gloved hands on his knees. His pale body is red from my blows, but he's blocking a lot better. He looks decent. We take our mouthguards out and drink some water. "What's gotten into you?"

"I always kick your ass."

"We had one fight!"

"And I won."

"You Trini?" he asks, out of nowhere.

Here we go.

Soon as a guy hears I'm from Trinidad, it's all over. Bam. Falls in love. I mean, not with me. With the idea that I can shake my ass better than a Jamaican and, as much as Trinis want to believe this, who can shake their ass better than a Jamaican? As good, yes. Better? This is a matter of serious debate. If he's looking for a dancehall queen, he better look somewhere else.

I slip my mouthguard in and grunt something in response. Let him only think I'm shaking my ass for him. I kiss my teeth. It doesn't have the desired effect because of the mouthguard. "Come on," I say, around the plastic. "Let's go another round."

We spar until he lands a swing kick good and proper into my ribs and I go down. Kru calls it then, looking at me all peculiar like. He says he's closing for the night and, true enough, when I look around we're the only people left in the gym.

I try not to smell him. Jason. But I still do. He still smells too good to be true.

"You look nice today," he tells me.

In my ripped tank top and third best pair of Thai shorts? The ones I have to roll down at the waist to get them to fit properly? Wow. Some people have no taste.

As we leave for the night, Jason turns to me and says, all casual, "I don't know why you lose so much when you fight. You're really good." Then he shrugs. "Must be a curse or something, Miss Trini."

I need this Mexican superstitious bullshit like I needed Mr. Abdi racially profiling me.

A curse.

Yeah, right.

thirteen

The day before Christmas holidays, Ma tells me that I'm going to work with Aunty K in New York for the break.

She barely looks at me when she breaks the news. She doesn't want to hear any backtalk from me, big surprise. The violence of a couple of nights ago is gone from her eyes, and so am I. In her mind, I'm not there right now. Not pleading to stay or anything. After the last day of class, I don't even have time to say bye to my lunchtime Desis, or my crew at the gym.

She's punishing me.

For the disobedience. For the fact that I've been nothing but a burden to her for all these years. For the questions that I wasn't supposed to ask Pammy about what she saw the night Dad died.

She drives me straight to the airport with some kind of Bollywood soundtrack blasting. She looks like something from out of a Bollywood film herself. She's flat-ironed her hair and put makeup on, dark streaks of eyeliner that should look garish but stop just short of that with a little upward tick, like a checkmark or the Nike logo. She's tried to teach me how to do this a few times but gives up when I inevitably look like a buff raccoon.

Sitting there beside her, I think about the last time we were in the car together. Even though she's doing her best to drown it all out with these Hindi songs, the sounds of a language she doesn't even speak.

Beyond the windshield, on the other side of the hood, is the front bumper and memories of a godawful sickening crunch that I can't ignore.

But she can.

Inside my suitcase is a packed lunch and snacks for the plane. It's a short flight and I don't need to be lugging all this food with me. I can feel her residual anger, but nothing will ever stop her from feeding me until I burst. When she leaves me at a security checkpoint, at the lineup before the gate, I hold her gaze and dump the food in the garbage. Tupperware included.

She doesn't blink.

Just stares at me until I go through the line and out of her sight. I can feel her eyes on me the whole way. That's okay with me. Let her look at Ravi like that. I spend the whole plane ride trying to not picture them together in the house while I'm away.

Aunty K starts chatting from the minute she meets me at JFK. It's like she's stored up conversations for weeks or something, just for me. "Why are you so quiet?" she keeps asking. On the train to her tiny apartment from the airport. At the apartment. When I'm on the sofa bed in the living room. The next morning when I start work at her cramped roti shop in Brooklyn.

She doesn't stop talking, doesn't stop asking. She makes the roti, someone named Mary fills it, and I handle the cash. All the loneliness she must feel living here by herself seems to be gone now with my stellar presence.

I turn my phone on after the first day and it starts buzzing right away.

Where are you? Noor.

Another buzz. Amanda. *Sparring 2nite?*

Jason, who got my number off the list at fight camp, sends me a photo from the demo where I dropped his ass. *Rematch? Fight prep? Where you at?*

Got a new gf so don't cry for me. Columbus.

Haha, I text him back. *Make sure you use a bike pump to inflate her or else your jaw'll get sore.*

That's what she said.

I know. I did.

Then I look at Jason's text. What do I say? I don't know, so I just tell him I'm in New York for the holidays. See him when I get back.

He sends me a thumbs-up. It could mean nothing. I mean, it probably means nothing. Right?

I work my ass off for these couple weeks. This is no Foot Locker, I'm telling you that. You think retail is bad? Try working at a roti shop in Brooklyn for less than minimum wage. Ma calls every day, but I refuse to talk to her. She put me here, left me to work under the table, washing dishes and coming back to a lumpy sofa bed every night with shitty soca songs looping in my head and smelling of Grade-B curry. Nothing I do can get the odor out of my hair. Nothing but the garbage that piles up out back when I haul out the restaurant trash. Garbage and curry are my life this break, and I know exactly what got me here.

I should have kept my mouth shut, like Ma told me. I should never have talked to Pammy about the night Dad died.

I feel my muscles slackening, going soft, turning to jelly, so I start running in the mornings. New York is going through the same kind of seasonal madness as Toronto, where there isn't a flake of snow to be found anywhere. It's . . . hot. Thank you, global warming. I go for runs so early the sun isn't even up yet. Aunty K bought me two rape whistles. Two. Just in case I get attacked and no one comes, I can chuck one at the guy and still have one to spare.

Aunty K likes books about Trinidad, is constantly talking about going back, though why she would ever is beyond me. A more fucked-up country I never even imagined. Thank God for Canada. I mean, we've got problems, but not Trinidad-level problems.

Now I know more than what could fill an A-cup sparkly bra with tassels. I'm up to a B-cup, at least. Aunty K's knowledge matches her actual cup size, which is bordering on an H. Christ.

"Richest country in the Caribbean," Aunty K says, shaking her head. Her hair has long streaks of gray that she doesn't bother to dye brown anymore. "Pitch, sugar cane, natural gas. Always drilling offshore. It's a curse. So much money there and everybody wants some. They don't care about nobody back home."

And don't get the roti-shop Trinis talking about the Venezuelans. The moaning about the effect of Venezuela's collapse on island life is almost a pastime. As if the Venezuelans did it on purpose!

On the top shelf of her bookcase are the family photo albums. Ma doesn't keep any at home because Aunty K started hoarding all the photos a long time ago. I take them out at night, one by one, and go through them. They're filled with images of life in Trinidad. By day I go to the roti shop and am surrounded by the West Indian diaspora and their shit talking, the way they sling acronyms like PNM, UNC, DDP, ILP, et cetera. The only thing I understand from the conversations is that Trinidad is the most dangerous place in the world, but also there is nowhere sweeter. In the minds of these immigrants, both of these things are true. The *tabanca* is real.

Tabanca, if you don't know, is a Trini way of saying you love something that doesn't love you back. The island pushed them out, but they still love it.

Nowhere else in the world you can walk to the corner and get a hot doubles, eat it right there on the road. Wash it down with an Apple J.

Where the women are so thick and beautiful you can't find the like anywhere else. (Although, trust me, never say that to a Bajan. All you're gonna get is an earful of Rihanna worship for your troubles.)

Where they are so strong you know they can handle whatever weight you lay on their shoulders.

Where they are so dangerous, you can never turn your back on them, not for a second. (The moment you do, they'll be flinging something at your head, telling people your business, generally messing up your life any which way they can.)

Aunty K comes into the den, which she uses as a second bedroom when I'm here. I've already put the photos away and I'm just trying to go to sleep, but I can't even have privacy for *that*. In her hands are those tiny cards you get at the paint store. She's looking at the brightest color samples, of course.

She switches on the lamp and announces that she's renovating the restaurant. "What do you think of these shades?" she asks, running a hand through her sharp new bob. Which is now dyed scarlet. A present that she gave herself yesterday. She ducked out of the shop for three hours and came back with a haircut and color that I never thought I'd see on her. Gone is the muted chestnut of her past and here she is, with a red crown and the matching lipstick.

Now, I've seen what we make at the restaurant. Over the years she's complained endlessly about how hard it is to survive in New York. But that must have changed, because she's thinking about a renovation. She looks at me, and smiles a strange little smile, an uncertain one. I think she's about to tell me something important, there's just that feeling of quiet that comes before . . . but the moment passes. She turns back to the sample cards.

"Which one do you like better?" she says instead.

I'm asked to choose between a yellow and an orange that both threaten to burn my retinas. So I go with the orange, because it's slightly more forgiving.

Ma calls on Christmas Day but I miss it because I'm too busy working at the shop. She doesn't leave a message. Later, Aunty K and I eat leftover roti for dinner and I unwrap a pair of gold earrings from them both. Dangly ones that are too pretty to even think about wearing. Aunty K gets a warm scarf from me. When she asks me what I got for Ma, I say "Nothing," because I didn't have time to get her anything before she packed me off and I'm still mad that I have to be here. Missing the gym Christmas party where we all get together wearing something other than tiny shorts. Not even going to Times Square for New Year's Eve improves my mood. On the packed train over there, Columbus texts me.

I think your mom is crying. Should I go over?

You can hear her? Is she alone?

Yeah, she's alone.

I think, good. *She wouldn't want you to see her like that. Where's your mom?*

Out.

Columbus is home alone on New Year's, and so is Ma. Where the hell is Ravi, though? I guess part of me thought that Ma sent me away not just for talking to Pammy but because she wanted to be with Ravi without me there. But it's not Ma's style at all to do something like that, and now I feel bad that she's alone. Even though it's her own fault. I try to call her but her phone is off. Every call goes to voicemail.

I can't get her out of my head.

On the way into Manhattan, I couldn't care less about the stupid countdown. Aunty K is still talking. Several times I try to tell her about Ma alone, crying, but there's something new and fragile about Aunty K right now. Like the red in her hair hasn't settled in on her yet and she's not really sure about it. She keeps fussing with the strands, pulling them forward and examining them. She seems close to tears, too, like maybe she's only just discovering she wasn't meant to be a ginger, so I shut my mouth and pretend to be interested in numbers being counted backward. At the stroke of midnight, she throws her arms around me and kisses me wetly on the cheek.

"Aunty!" I push her away and wipe the lipstick mark off my face.

"Oh, live a little," she says. Which is rich, coming from her. I don't need advice from a fifty-year-old spinster on how to live. I think she must have read the thought in my mind, in the witchy new way of hers. She turns quiet on the train ride back. Everyone in our carriage is strangely subdued, too, except for a couple having a hushed fight at the opposite end of the car. It's like Aunty K's mood has expanded outward like a force field and has knocked everyone into some kind of examination of their life choices.

Or maybe thinking about a whole new year of the same shit does this to everyone. People talk about the New York magic, but I dunno, it feels dark here. Like everyone thinks it'll be like something out of a film and it's never what you expect.

Columbus and Noor text me to say Happy New Year, so I text them back. After two minutes of thinking about it, I text Jason, too. I get a fireworks emoji from him, like right away. I know it's silly and I shouldn't think anything about it, but it feels nice.

fourteen

Ma picks me up from the airport and she doesn't have a whole lot to say besides asking me how my flight was and whether or not I'm hungry. She's quiet and I don't want to be bringing up anything that will send me back to the roti shop, so I just keep my mouth shut until we get home.

She pulls into the parking lot and turns off the car. I'm about to get out but she stops me. "Trisha, I have to talk to you about something."

For a moment I think she's going to bring up Dad, but then she says, "Ravi is going to be around more often. I know you don't like him, but I think you should give him a chance."

I think she *shouldn't* give him a chance, since he ditched her on New Year's. She gets out of the car before I can reply.

It takes me a while to follow her into the townhouse, which has always been her space. Never mine. Even when Ma's not there, her presence spreads like bacteria after a sweltering July day at the gym. It's everywhere. In the furniture she's chosen, the colors on the wall, right down to the arrangement of the dishes in the cupboard. Even my father, when he was alive, was careful to leave as small an impression as possible on her house, since he lived half the year knocking about in Trinidad anyway.

But now there's Ravi, and his presence feels like a more permanent thing.

When I go inside, there he is. Fixing the back door. "I already did that," I say, as I grab clean hand wraps from the clothesline.

"You did it wrong. I should have fixed this weeks ago."

He digs through his toolkit for something. "I knew I broke it when I came in," he says absently. "Damn flimsy thing."

I stare at him. "You're the one who broke the lock on the back door?"

He freezes. "I hear your mother calling you. You better go see what she wants." He says this easily, like I'm going to forget about this anytime soon. Ravi broke our back door trying to get inside, even before he and Ma got together.

Around the time Dad died.

What the hell is happening here?

"Ma," I say, when I get upstairs. She's in the kitchen, heating up some lunch. "Ravi's the one who broke the back door—"

She slams a pot down on the counter. "Trisha, I swear if you bring up that door again, you won't be going to that gym for the rest of the school year."

"But—"

"I mean it!"

This is so ridiculous! But effective. She really knows how to get to me sometimes.

Fine.

I ask her if by saying Ravi's going to be around more often, she means he's living here now and if he's got a job to go to maybe?

"Yes, he's here now. And he works at a warehouse." She sighs and turns away from me.

I've never seen her so tired. I get the feeling that Ravi keeps her up a lot at night, but I don't really want to think about that, because ew.

I find out later his part-time warehouse job is in Mississauga, where he operates a forklift. When he's not doing that, he's shirtless on the couch, his saggy chest sprouting new hairs every day. My father was no peach in that department either (too much roti and fried rice can do that to a person), but at least he kept his shirt on.

And apparently we have an accident at his work to thank for Ravi's constant presence in our house.

Using up all the hot water in the mornings. Replacing my whey protein with a disgusting vegan version, on account of his old-man digestive issues. Looking at my biceps with judgment, as though they're puny. Which, of course, they're not, because even though the trip to New York has me off my regular training regimen, I'm working my chin-up bar and I can lift like a motherfucker. Well, myself. Still. Lifting yourself like a motherfucker is no small feat.

"What's up with this Ravi guy?" asks Columbus, the day after I return. We're on his bed, as per usual now that Ravi is a constant fixture in my house. Tomorrow is our first day back at school from break. We don't talk too much at school, so Columbus likes to get in these little chat sessions outside of class time. "Why is he always there? Doesn't he have his own place to go to?"

"No, he's moved in for good," I say, beyond depressed about this. "He hurt his back a couple years ago. A crate fell on him at work or something. So apparently he needs a lot of rest, according to my mom."

"Shoulda fell on him harder," mutters Columbus. No shit. It's about the first time Columbus has been right about anything. "So what about New York? Any hookups?" he asks, abruptly changing the subject.

"No."

He rubs his puny pecs. "Not even some up-top action? Christmas holidays before college and you're in New York City?"

Which, to Columbus, is like hookup central because he's never actually been.

"Don't worry," he says, with one of his baby punches to my shoulder. "You'll get laid in college. But it's kinda pathetic, still."

Apparently he spent his break having butt loads of sex with a (slightly) older woman who worked at the accessory store at the mall. She is, as he put it delicately, a fine piece of ass, a Guyanese import (who likes her men skinny and barely legal, I guess). If Columbus is telling the truth, which is up for debate.

"I gotta go train," I say, pushing him off the bed.

"Right," he says, as I step over him. "You know real men don't like women with muscles."

"When I see a real man, I'll ask him."

But it bothers me all the way to the gym. I see Ricky at reception and bring up my demo fight with Jason, making sure to comment on his cardio. Naturally, Ricky takes this opportunity to tell me everything he knows about Jason. College boy. Training for less than a year. Has "heart." Lives in res but comes back to the east end most weekends to do his laundry at home.

"Girlfriend?" I ask.

Ricky smirks. "Why do you want to know?"

"Why don't you want to say?"

"Lucky wants to get lucky," Ricky teases. "Lucky" is what they call me as a private joke since I never win my fights. He's about to say some other douchebag thing but shuts up quick because Kru comes into the reception area just then.

Kru smiles when he sees me, asks about my holiday. I feel like all my dreams have come true for just that moment.

I don't tell him about the roti shop or hanging out with my aunt. I tell him about my morning runs and the shadow-boxing I did to keep sharp. He gives me a round of pads and shakes his head sadly at the end. "You need work."

So I'm back to training every day.

Kru has me hold pads for the little kids in the junior class and it's not so bad because at least he gives me a round or two after evening sessions. I feel an itch, just beneath my skin. Sparring isn't the same, it really isn't. I need the ring. The crowd. The feeling of surrender to what is happening between me and the other girl.

Like my mother, who has completely surrendered to Ravi. She's so busy all the time now, with work and dealing with him. Even my eighteenth birthday wasn't anything special. Just some takeout and a cake. She looked relieved that I didn't want any presents, only money. Usually she loves shopping for me, but I'm kind of glad I have no more dresses taking up room in my closet. I'm okay with not spending time at the house now that Ravi's there. In fact, I prefer it.

One night I come home so late they don't know what to do with me. It wasn't my fault. Sparring went past closing time and Ricky was the one closing so he didn't bother kicking us out the way that Kru would have.

When I get to the house, I try to be quiet. Ravi comes into the kitchen while I mix a protein shake. He knocks the tub out of my hand. A puff of vanilla-scented powder comes flying up at us.

"We have rules here now," he says, as the container rolls away and into the wall. "This door locks at nine o'clock. No more gallivanting around till all hours of the night, you hear? That's not what proper young ladies do."

I do hear, but I kinda zone him out because who ever told him I was a proper young lady, anyway? My attention is focused on Ma. She's standing behind him, a stricken look on her face. This is new, so very fresh that we're both reeling from it. She has never, not once, allowed my father to speak to me like this because it's always been understood that I'm hers, and hers alone. To love, to scold, to whatever.

But she stands silent behind Ravi and lets him.

She lets him.

fifteen

Proper young lady, my backside. I'll show him. I start training so hard that, before I know it, I've got an injury of my own to deal with. I sprain my right ankle. It hurts like a bitch, but just a little whiny one. I've sprained this ankle before, so it's always a little off. On the floor, I double up on the compression sleeve and am careful to only work my right swing kick on the bag, so that I'm pivoting only on the left leg for now. I make sure the kicks are mid-thigh so that there's no chance of over-extending and catching a bit of the ankle by mistake.

"What's wrong with you?" says Jason, as he walks past. Shirtless. He's been watching me a lot since I got back, out of the corner of his eye. "You look rusty, Lucky." But I can still beat him one-on-one, so there's that. Luckier than him, at least.

"Yeah, well, you look soft," I say.

He grins, passes a hand down his abs. He's got six of them. I've counted. "Soft, huh?"

Amanda smirks because she's pure muscle. Noor shakes her head at him in mock pity as he grabs his gear and heads off to the men's locker room. I wonder, again, if he's got a girlfriend. If he doesn't, I may have ruined my chance with him with that soft comment.

Do I even want a chance with him?

I never really bother with guys because . . . okay . . . I mean . . . it just never was right or whatever . . .

But Jason.

It's not really about his abs, because I have some of my own. So. His are nice but they aren't the deciding factor. Maybe I like that he's already in college. Am I into mature men?

Gross.

It could just be Jason. I think about how good he smells.

This time I have the good sense to keep these thoughts to myself. Ricky's not around to tease me, but you never know. He could be hiding behind the weights or whatever, just waiting for an opportunity to jump out and say something annoying. I honestly don't know what Amanda sees in him.

When Jason's gone, we chat for a bit and then we spar.

It's beautiful. So beautiful. Nothing like it in the world. We don't even care that the gym smells like ass today, because we're all a bit ripe after we've been at it for so long. I don't mind the smell. It may be rank with ass, but it's our ass. There's a fresh bruise on my thigh, shining deep purple, aching all the way down to the bone. I pour some bright orange Thai liniment on it and rub the heel of my hand over it until the pain evens out to a steady throb. With my team around me, stretching and slap-sparring with their gear off, I feel pure, whole.

I never want this moment to end.

I get back home just before nine so no one can complain. Then I wait till they're asleep (which is how I think of Ma and Ravi now: them) and rummage through the medicine cabinet. There's usually a bottle of Advil somewhere. I search the whole bathroom but all I see is four little vials stashed under the sink in a pouch that wasn't there before. Glass vials with a white label that says *fentanyl citrate*, clear as day. I get this funny feeling again, like I did at Dad's funeral, and when Ma brought Ravi home. This is wrong. The vials shouldn't be here. Aren't people dying left, right and center in our hood from fentanyl?

But here they are.

Ma doesn't really talk about her work, and she definitely doesn't bring it home, so I'm standing there wondering what the hell medication that looks like it's from the hospital is doing here until someone pounds on the door.

"Hurry up!" calls Ravi.

I open the door to find him standing there with his arms crossed. He's shirtless, *quelle surprise*.

(Why, God? Why do you do this to me?)

So I'm extra careful not to brush past him. Something's wrong with him; I can see it in his eyes. Like he's just taken a jab to the face and needs a minute to shake it off. "What you looking at?" he says to me, with a sneer. But it comes slow, like he's underwater.

I slide past him, no problem. "Nothing," I say, as I go to my room. I'm not scared of him, but I can't help but wonder who put those little vials underneath the sink. I thought my dad was a bad influence on Ma, I really did.

I think Ravi might be something worse.

When I creep downstairs the next morning, I see Ravi's duffel bag on the sofa. He's nowhere to be found. The bag is open. There's a phone peeking out. One that looks pretty familiar, an older model . . . but it can't be whose I think it is.

I reach for it and turn it on.

While I'm waiting for it to boot up, I see a little baggie of pills in the duffel. Each pill is imprinted with the initials TEC. After the vials, it feels wrong, this whole thing, so I put the phone and the baggie back and am about to leave when I hear it.

The beat of a steel pan coming from Ravi's bag, playing a very familiar song.

I recognize that ring tone. That old calypso. It's "Bassman."

I slip the ringing phone into my own bag and leave as quickly as I can. I run all the way to the bus stop. When the bus comes and I get on, I can't help but look back to see if anyone else is springing down the street after me.

Then I pull out the phone. It's Dad's.

I don't recognize the number that called right when I turned it on, but that doesn't really matter so much because what I do know is that somehow, Ravi had my dad's phone.

The next day I look for the little vials, but they're not under the sink anymore. I want to ask Ma where they are, but she's already gone and there's no way I'm going to initiate a conversation with Ravi. Besides, I don't want to let him know what I found, because then he might wonder if I know about the pills in his bag, which I do. According to Ricky, TEC is how you identify bootleg painkillers on the streets. I know he got hurt at his warehouse job, so maybe that's why he's got to take pills?

Speaking of painkillers, there's still no Advil, so I go to school on an ankle that feels like it's on fire.

After class, I'm walking home from the bus stop when a car pulls up beside me. The window rolls down. I start walking faster, but then I hear Columbus's voice. "Get in!" he shouts, a huge smile on his pimply face. He's leaning out the window of a silver Honda Civic from about a decade ago.

"When did you get a car?" I say.

"Mom bought it for me this afternoon. Paid for the whole thing in cash, like a boss." The potential sexiness he maybe had for a second disappears. I think about poor Pammy, having to buy his car for him.

"How much was it?"

"She wouldn't let me see. A few Gs, I think. But I've got to pay the insurance, she says, so I'm thinking delivery. If you want to chip in, I'll add you on the policy," he offers.

I sense a trap. Besides, how much does insurance cost on an old car like this? But I tell him I'll think about it as I get in.

When Ma comes home later, she's tired but starts to put dinner on anyway, even though I told her I already ate. I'm shocked that she's cooking. It's like Dad isn't even gone. She comes home dead tired and there's a man to be taken care of. The good thing about Dad was that he was only here for a couple months at a time.

But Ravi doesn't go anywhere.

I disappear upstairs, saying I've got too much homework to sit around the table, but in reality I just don't want to look at Ravi's smug face a second longer than I have to.

When they go to bed, I go downstairs for a glass of water and on the way back to my room, pause outside Ma's bedroom. I can't think of it as theirs yet. I hear Ravi's voice. He's saying something about St. James, the place in Trinidad where Ma grew up. I only hear snatches from him—his voice is too low for anything else—but from what I can make of it he's talking about an old man's parrot. The day the old man died in his grocery store, the parrot shouted "Eliza is a whore!"

over and over until someone came in and discovered the body. No one knew who Eliza was, but it fuelled the village gossip mill for years.

Ma, when she speaks, I can hear better. Even the exhaustion in her voice. "Yes, Ravi, I remember. I was with you when we got the news. How could I forget?"

There are shuffling sounds, like someone's getting out of bed. I'm safely back in my room by the time Ma's door opens. I've heard that parrot story before, and I can't get over Ma saying she was with Ravi when it happened.

The only person I can ask about the story is Aunty K. She's probably asleep now, though. I'll just have to call her tomorrow.

sixteen

Kru is proud of his female fighters. Even me, with my matchstick wrists and my losing streak. The fighters camp is his elite group and there are only a handful of girls in it. He takes me, Noor and Amanda aside today, real serious, and tells us about the tournament in Florida for girls only. We're too excited to pretend we're not.

"Florida?"

"Where all the old people are?"

"Is there prize money?"

"I thought Florida was under water? I mean, not the whole thing, but climate change—"

"What are the fees?"

"Don't people wrestle alligators down there? I hear the Florida dudes are whack."

"But, seriously, is there prize money?"

He puts his hand up and we fall silent. "Florida, in May. You have to sign up now and we start training. There is no prize money. Are you in?"

We look at each other, at Kru, and then, one by one, nod. He's asking us if we're serious. We've never been more serious about anything in our lives. The guy fighters at the gym look on, overrun with jealousy. The Montreal tournament got canceled last minute when one of the organizers absconded with everyone's fee money. It hurt to lose that much cash but even more to be training for nothing.

And now, Kru and the female fighters, we have something that's just ours.

So hell yeah. I'm going to Florida, where all the whack dudes and old people are.

Florida is on my mind so much it takes me a couple days to call Aunty K. Her surprise at getting my call doesn't stop her from talking non-stop for about three minutes before she finally says "Trisha, girl, I was just thinking about you. Want to come up for a week and help out at the store for March Break?"

Do I want to work for minimum wage during my break, infusing my skin and hair with the smell of curry, or do I want to spend it with Ma and freaking Ravi?

"Yeah, I can come," I say, after zero thought.

After that, she's in a good mood. So am I, actually. I hadn't thought about what I was going to do for that week, but at least it's been sorted. "I'm reading this book on Trinidad and it got me thinking," I say. "There was a story you told me once about an old man who died and a parrot kept shouting some stuff so that people would open the door and find the body."

"Eliza and the parrot? That's your mom's story, not mine," Aunty K replies.

"Oh, yeah? I couldn't remember. How long ago did it happen?"

"Twenty years now? Something like that. Your mommy must have been around sixteen, I think. So listen, give me the dates of your break and I'll book the ticket for you."

"Okay, Aunty," I say, before letting her continue chatting for another few minutes. She'd decided to ignore my advice on the paint and went with the yellow instead. "Brighter," she says.

Yeah, so bright you could go blind from it.

The next day in World Issues class—

Why is World Issues a prereq for Business Management, anyway?

Who the hell actually knows?

—I start thinking about how the people around me are changing. Ma with Ravi, Aunty K with her expansion. Everyone but Columbus, who's exactly the same but with a new (old) car.

Pammy buying him a car in cash, though. That's something different.

Ever since her divorce, she's been teaching Columbus the value of hard work and saving. All that jazz. Her ex was kind of a deadbeat and she wants to make sure Columbus doesn't become one, too. Plus, she works as a dental hygienist. She does okay, but it's not like she makes tons of money. I mean, not enough for that car and also to save for his tuition next year—which I know she does.

I mention the car to Ma later that night at the dinner table, but she changes the subject.

Ravi talks a bit after that about how single women spoil their children too much and this is why they're always broke. Ma looks uncomfortable and changes the subject again. I don't know why. She loves to gossip about Pammy, even though they're best friends. Pammy's life is something of a mystery to her, I think. Pammy kicking her ex out the way she did. Putting her foot down the way she did.

Must sting for Ma because she never had the courage to get rid of Dad. She just kept taking the beats until he died.

"You're a wound," Ravi continues, because I guess he thinks we want to hear what he has to say on the subject. "You women. Press on you just a little and you all just scream. Give everything up."

And Ma's boiling, she's so furious. Ravi is slow as usual. He doesn't pick up on it, but I do. The sudden anger. I wait for her to whip something at him, to get up with a burst of energy and shout at him. Every now and then I'd seen her do this with Dad, though she always got in trouble for it later.

But letting a comment like that pass?

I'm confused, then I'm frightened because it seems that Jason was right. I'm cursed. I'm doomed. It's never going to change with her, except I catch a glimpse of something under the table. It's her hand, clenched around a fork, pressing the tines into her thigh. She sees me looking but doesn't stop.

"Ma," I say. There's something dangerous about her right now.

Ravi frowns. "I don't know what's wrong with the two of you today." He leaves the room, pressing his hand into the small of his back like a pregnant lady.

It's only after he's gone that she puts the fork back on the table and massages the imprint she's made on her thigh.

Ravi falls asleep on the couch, which is a normal thing now, I guess, and I hear Ma moving about in her bedroom. I think about Dad's phone in the front pocket of my backpack, where I keep it now, and I want to ask her why it was in Ravi's bag. Did she give it to him?

It doesn't make any sense.

The questions are there, just waiting to spill out.

I pause just outside of the room because I can hear her voice now. The door's closed, but I listen anyway. She's talking real quiet to Pammy, like always, but this time it's charged. Something in her voice is so determined and so powerful that I can't believe she let anybody ever knock her about. That she'd let Ravi talk down to her like that. Maybe this power is new. Maybe my dad's death is feeding it somehow, because I feel it strong, and feel something in me rise up to meet it.

The fear, you know, the fear in me doesn't ever go away.

seventeen

"I mean," Columbus begins, "you sure it's a good idea to go for a driving test right now?"

"They said I wasn't at fault for the accident, okay?"

"*Okay*, but the last time you drove, a man died." Columbus isn't exactly known for his tact, but still. It's pretty rude of him to bring it up.

"Are you going to lend me your junk car or not?"

"With that kind of attitude . . . Look, I'm not saying you're a terrible driver, but you're a terrible driver and maybe you need some time to not be as terrible as you clearly are."

Since we're already on our way to the test center, I ignore this. It's my last test before I get my full license.

I'm not nervous until I'm outside waiting for the guy giving the test. He saunters out to the back lot where I'm parked. I take in his baby face, the sparse mustache that's trying to crawl across his lip but not succeeding, and I know that it's not going to go well for me.

I start off okay, up until the ramp to the highway, then the panic sets in. He's judging everything I do, checking things off with a flick of his pencil. I speed up and put my signal on, see another car coming up fast before I merge . . .

I scream and pump the brakes hard.

We both go slamming forward into our seatbelt then back to the seat.

"Put on your hazards," he says. Now he's looking at me for real, like I just tried to kill him, which I guess is a reasonable position to take.

We switch seats, and he drives us back to the test center because I'm a blubbering mess. Columbus is waiting for me in the seating area. The grin on his face dies when he sees me come in with the examiner. I'm still shaking. Columbus pats me awkwardly on the back but, for once, knows better than to say anything.

Word gets out that I'm officially a menace on the road. Nobody's all that surprised. Aunty K calls to talk to me about it but ends up blaming Dad for everything that went wrong with my life and Ma's. "That monster. He's taken so much from your childhood, Trisha, and now he takes this milestone, too."

Um. Okay, Aunty.

Ravi offers to give me driving lessons, but I stare at him so hard that he turns back to the television and continues to ignore me for the rest of the day, until Ma gets home. Then he decides he's got to be elsewhere, for once.

Now it's just the two of us.

She comes downstairs, her hair still wet from the shower, and makes us some tea. With steaming mugs at our sides, I sit between her legs and let her rub coconut oil into my hair, separating it into sections and working the oil lightly through the strands, the way she used to do all the time when I was a kid. She doesn't do it as much anymore, so it feels especially nice. Her back is to the window, a stream of sunlight warming her. "Ahh," she sighs, stretching her fingers up into the light before returning them to me. "Only way to dry your hair is in the sun."

It never gets old, hearing this.

"We'll schedule another test soon," she says, after a moment. "We should have waited a bit, anyway."

"There's a fee this time. If you don't pass and have to take it again."

"Don't worry about that, baby." Her voice as light as the fingertips that graze through my scalp. She pulls my hair into a French braid that snakes down my back. The sun dims around us, the tea cools.

I sink into the feeling, relaxing so much I'm almost asleep when I say: "Do you ever wish you didn't have me, Ma? How your life would have been?"

For a moment, I'm not sure if she's heard me. "Never,"

she says, breathing into my hair, the stream of air from her nose tickling my scalp. Then she kisses my forehead, just at the edge of my hairline, transferring the warmth she collected from the sunshine to me. I feel like a kid again, but that's alright, especially after the day I had. "Let's order some dinner. What do you want?"

"But it's not the end of the month."

She laughs. "We can make an exception this one time. Let's order. Your choice."

After the Thai food arrives, she transfers some money to me, more than I've ever seen in my bank account. More than I need to reschedule the test, anyway. Whatever, I'm not going to complain. There's end-of-the-month takeout in my belly and we're still a couple weeks away from that treat. I failed my test and Ma, she's showing me she'll take care of me no matter what. The kiss on my forehead is still warm. It spreads through me, warming me throughout the night and as I fall into sleep.

I guess I shouldn't be surprised when the nightmares come, though. Shows how stupid I am. The screech of the tires. The thud along the bumper. The darkness. The rain. Dad's face. A busted lip. A broken back door with the wind whistling through. The sun nowhere to be found.

It's so cold.

I wake up shivering and feel a roiling in my belly, the heavy meal I ate before bed sitting like a boulder.

If he was a monster, what does that make me?

eighteen

I'm usually out all day but as long as I'm back by 9 p.m., King Ravi can't say anything.

Training isn't going great, though I try to be there four to five times a week. Florida is going to be hot and humid, so we have to make sure our conditioning is on point or else we're chum. My conditioning is tight, but my technique is off. Kru said so last pad session, as rivers of sweat poured off me. He said my head isn't in the game, shouted it, and I was so embarrassed I didn't stick around afterwards like I usually do. Every day we're in, Kru has us on the basics to make sure that no matter how dead we are, we'll never forget the essentials.

One, two, slip is what I work on today. Over and over, until it feels like it'll be in my memory forever.

After you come in with the jab and cross, you've got to make sure you're anticipating their next move, their next punch. That's why the slip is so important. And after you slip, your right cross comes in strong.

That's the whole point of it.

You slip, you fake, you dodge, you let them think one thing while you're setting them up for another.

When Dad died, the police should have been on the look-out for a fake, but a car full of distraught women on a rainy night? Please. They didn't stand a chance. Especially when Pammy came out in hysterics and threw her arms around me and started bawling into my shoulder "Poor baby. Poor, poor baby. Your dad—he's with the angels now!"

I think even Columbus was shocked when he heard about that part. Pammy in hysterics? Going on about freaking angels? Crazy talk. Except it did happen and I've got the beige foundation stains on my jacket to prove it.

I'm with Columbus in his kitchen, eating takeaway jerk chicken, when Pammy comes in from work in her scrubs. "Good to see you both still have an appetite what with all that homework you've got on," she says, nibbling on a leg Columbus passes to her.

Why wouldn't we have an appetite?

She sits, eats silently with us and then looks at the hole in the sleeve of my sweater as though she's never seen anything like it in the world before. "Trisha, how old is this thing?" she exclaims, plucking at the tear with her manicured fingers. "Tell your mom to give you some of that insurance money to buy yourself some new clothes, for God's sake!"

It takes a few moments for this to sink in.

Columbus looks at me. "What insurance money?"

"Don't worry about it," I say, just to piss him off. But I'm wondering the same thing. I glance over at Pammy, who has gotten up and left the room without another word to us.

"What's up with your ma?" I ask Columbus.

He frowns, then shrugs. "She's been weird lately. Did you see her nails?"

I did. Pammy with a manicure. Also with a little flash of diamonds at her ears when she pulls her hair back. Buying a car, even a used one, with cash. When Columbus isn't looking, I open the cupboard above the kettle again. Still no chamomile tea. And Pammy hasn't just been weird lately. She's been weird since the night Dad died. Since the angels comment.

"What are you doing over March Break?" Columbus asks.

"Going to New York to see Aunty K." Which reminds me. I need to get my passport from Ma.

"Can I come with?"

"There's no room at her place, and plus, you wouldn't want to. Trust me."

Ravi has the weekend off, so I wait until Monday to go into Ma's room to look for the little fireproof box she keeps in her closet. I need my passport but I'm also wondering about what Pammy said, something about insurance. Ma keeps all the important stuff in that box, so maybe there's some kind of explanation for Pammy's comment.

The box isn't there.

I search everywhere and eventually find it in the basement, under some old clothes. I take the key she gave me for it in case anything happened and open it up. It's empty. No birth papers, passports, bank documents, nothing. Not even my baby jewelery is in there, the little gold bangles and necklaces with shiny black beads that all Trinidadian Indian babies get from relatives when they're born. Aunty K bought me mine.

"She probs doesn't trust Ravi. That's why she hid the important stuff. My dad does the same thing," says Amanda the next day.

We've all put on a few pounds in the past couple weeks. Florida seems so far away right now. Hard to think about May when we're still dealing with the February freeze. No fights coming up and food is too good to give it up for nothing. Amanda looks better than me and Noor with the extra weight, though, as it's all gone to her ass. We're stuck with face and belly, which reminds me to stop eating so much. I wouldn't mind so much if it was boobs. At least Noor has boobs.

"For real," adds Noor. "My parents have a safe they keep things in."

Why would she be with him if she doesn't trust him?

"Dick," whispers Columbus later that night, on the phone. "He gives it to her good."

"That's disgusting."

"What? Why else would a woman like your mom put up with all that crap?"

"What do you mean, a woman like my mom?"

"Trish, your mom is fine. You know that right?"

Of course I do. Ma is the most beautiful woman in the world. Her eyes don't work so good, though. That's why she always ends up with these losers.

Pushing thoughts of Ravi and Ma from my mind, I close my eyes and picture Jason doing abs today, which even though he was covered in sweat, didn't seem gross at all. I thought the lunchtime Desis had killed my desire for guys completely. What with their talk of honor killings and getting shipped back if they got caught with a boy. I know one girl who actually did get tossed screaming onto a plane back to India. Everyone at school saw her making out with her boyfriend in the hallways, and someone had ratted her out. She had an army of cousins, who she swore were basically chill, but clearly one of them was *not* because one day she was moaning with us about some dumb assignment or another and the next she was gone.

No one, not even the cousins, ever heard from her again.

If I got knocked up in high school, I have no doubt Ma would ship me back to live with some obscure relative in Trinidad, no problem, to pay for my mistake. But it's not something I usually worry about, and plus, I'm not the kind of girl guys at my school usually go for. Not the soft, nice ones. I get looks, sure, but not the kind you're thinking. My legs are thick as tree trunks and just as hard. They're monsters. Pure muscle. They can take a swing kick, brace and return in a matter of seconds. Split seconds. The fast-twitch fibers in my calves can catapult me into motion as quick as you can blink, and then I'm on you. One, two, grab, knee, clinch, push, step in, elbow. A matter of seconds, not even.

"You only think it's gross cuz you never had any dick," Columbus says, reminding me he's still on the line. "I know a guy, if you want to find out more?"

"Is he skinny with zits all over his face? Because thanks, no thanks."

He hangs up, letting me know that yeah, it totally was a skinny guy with acne. Columbus is so obvious sometimes. Am I a desperate Guyanese retail worker at the mall? Please.

At the gym.

We're clinching.

I hate it so much even though I get a desperate little thrill whenever I'm in control. Clinching is all about fighting your opponent for the crown of the head, the plum, and pulling it down just as you extend the knee up. Your job is to protect your head while getting a hold on the other guy and kneeing him in the face. Brutal, but this sport ain't for wusses. Clinching is all about the neck, so to get us stronger, Kru has us put on a leather head mask thingie that makes you look like a character from a horror movie. You're supposed to strap weights on the bottom and then move your head up and down to make your neck stronger.

"Blow job practice," says Noor, as she straps herself in.

I wait until my turn and feel like an idiot while I jerk my head up and down. Out of the corner of my eyes, I see Jason watching me from the chin-up station, looking at me like he doesn't mind my thick legs. So I do it some more, even slower. He watches the whole time. I wonder if his dick is good—

What's good dick, anyway? Like, specifically?

—even though I'm trying to focus.

A few minutes later our gloves are off and we're clinching.

It's only me, Amanda and Noor until Jason joins us to partner me. I guess he thinks he's helping out, even though he's actually the worst at clinching. We start slap-sparring until one of us pulls the other in. I feel his arms come around me, not in a clinch, really. His form is terrible, but I don't care about that right now. And when he sneaks a hand up to my head, it pauses at the base of my neck and brushes the little hairs there. We're both sweating and as we pull toward each other, I feel him hard against my thigh.

He disengages and walks off the mats to the washroom. I think he's embarrassed until he sends me a little smile. A little flutter of warmth spreads from my lower stomach and I feel this ache between my legs. Like, it hurts even. I feel full and empty at the same time. What the actual fuck?

I wonder, did he do that on purpose?

Kru leaves for the night, leaving Ricky to lock up. It's only the fighters left, anyway. Ricky plays a clip from a gym in Thailand, where two fighters are conditioning with blows to the body. No gloves, wraps, wrist or ankle guards. They deliver and take hit after hit, until red splotches show on their brown bodies. So we do a bit of that, too. Jason stays away from me, either because he doesn't want to hit me like that, or he doesn't want to repeat what happened in clinching.

We leave, one by one. I wait for him in the parking lot. Noor and Amanda have gone home, both laughing at me before they left because it seems like everyone knows what's up. Jason sees me from the door and smiles again, but I can tell he's nervous. He keeps wiping his palms against his jeans. We walk to the train station together.

One moment we're just talking and the next we're kissing by the entrance of the station.

His lips are softer than I expected them to be, but I kinda like it. Okay, I more than like it. Here I am, now an eighteen-year-old virgin being kissed by a college boy.

I highly recommend it.

Eventually we say goodbye. I think about Jason all the way home. I'm unable to do my economics homework for the rest of the night. I can't even think about Florida. That's how spun I am. I want more, but there's too much going on to ache this much. Right?

I can't do homework. I can't sleep. So I turn Dad's phone on. I haven't really wanted to before this. There was so much about Dad's life he kept from us that I'm just used to him being a bit of a mystery. I plug it into my charger because the battery is low and scroll through his messages. The steel pan blares from it, jarring me into motion. I answer the call quickly, but I don't say anything.

"Hello?" says a male voice. "Who is this?" He sounds uncertain, his Trini accent like molasses. Like a thick, dark melody, running slow.

I almost hang up the phone, but something crazy in me doesn't want to just yet. "Trisha. Who is this?"

"Junior."

It's a name I've heard whispered my whole life. Somebody important in Dad's world, who I never got to meet. Who Ma never wanted me to.

"Why are you calling? Dad is dead," I say.

There's a pause and I start to regret ever picking up the phone. "I know that. I call every so often to hear his voice on the message system. Sometimes I call for you."

Junior. This person who's been in Dad's life for almost as long as I have. I know Ma would be so pissed if she knew I was talking to someone in Dad's other family. The one he kept down on the island.

This time I do hang up.

I turn off the phone and toss it in my gym bag where nobody in their right mind would ever go looking.

Tonight was a big night for me. I kissed a college boy who can't fight and I also talked to my half-brother, Dad's first-born, for the first time in my life.

nineteen

So women are more likely to be murdered by their husbands or boyfriends than anyone else—

But what about the other way around?

—which I learned today in World Issues class, which I also didn't do my homework for. A test is coming up and I've got to do better. If I flunk and it brings down my average . . . I can't even imagine what Ma will do to me if she hears.

There's no time to train this week. So much studying. Dad's phone is in the locker at my gym now, buried far back, behind all the rank gear I've abandoned over the years. I store my half-brother Junior back there, too. I'm not ready to deal with him yet. I don't know if I'll ever be ready.

On my breaks, I look for the papers missing from the fireproof box everywhere I can but, finally, I have to do it. We're alone in the kitchen, and it's Ma's day off. I don't know where Ravi is. She looks happy for once, like she's in a decent mood. Painting her nails, something that she hardly does anymore.

Now or never.

"Why are you looking at me like that?" she asks. "If you're not busy, you could clean something for once, you know."

Which is insane, cuz I clean more than she does. If anyone needs to clean more, it's King Ravi. "I need my passport. Where did you put all our important stuff?"

"What do you need your passport for?"

"To check the expiry date. Going for March Break with Aunty K."

"She did mention something about that, you know. I think you have at least another year on that passport," she says, still not looking up.

"Can I just check, Ma?" I try not to sound like a brat, but I do. Besides, she's always telling me thinking isn't knowing. So. And I need to know for March Break in a few weeks, but also for Florida. "Aunty K already bought me the plane ticket and I don't want to let her down."

Finally, she looks at me. I have her complete attention now. "Alright, alright. Since when do you like going to work at her shop so much, anyway?"

"Since you sent me there at Christmas, Ma." This comes out a lot angrier than I wanted it to, but there's nothing I can do about that now.

She frowns, probably not buying that I suddenly developed a love for smelling like curry 24/7. And I'm pretty sure she wants me to say something about her and Ravi, like she's digging for info on how I feel, but I'm not in the mood. It's enough having him around. I legit don't even want to talk about him on top of having to look at his face. "Ma! My passport."

"Fine. I'll have to get it for you. We'll go to the bank later today."

"The bank?"

"I put everything in a safe deposit box."

"Since when?" I say.

Just like that her good mood's gone, too. She challenges me with her stare. "Since I felt like it. You want your passport or not?"

When we reach the bank, I'm out of the car as soon as it stops. I head into the tiny reception area so she won't have any excuse to leave me in the car. She mutters the box number 4242 when we get to the front of the line and it takes a few minutes until we're led to a room in the back. "Shouldn't I have a key, too?" I ask, as we walk down the narrow hall.

"Keep pushing it, Trisha, and see if you get to go to New York at all."

"But it's my papers in there, too, right? What if something happens to you and I need to get something from the box?"

"What's going to happen to me?" she says, suddenly fierce.

"I dunno. An accident, maybe. Like Dad . . ."

She ignores me and goes into the room first. The door slams in my face.

When she comes out about a minute later, grinning, I know she did it on purpose, closing me out like that. I take the passport and walk off ahead of her. I wait at the car for a good ten minutes before she leaves the bank, still sporting that stupid grin on her face. "Oh, fix your face," she says, when we're both in the car. "I put your name on the box, so if you need to get your birth papers and all that, all you need is the key."

I'm still mad, even though I got exactly what I asked for. "Can I have the key?"

"No." But that settles it, according to her.

I'm happy, too.

I've just seen her put the key in the leopard-print makeup bag she keeps in the glove compartment.

The next day Aunty K shows up and says she'll be here for just the weekend. I don't know why. I was supposed to go and see her for March Break, which is in just a few weeks. That's what the big deal about the passport was for. She said she got someone to run the shop while she's away. I get the sense that something's happening with her and Ma. Pammy seems to know about it, too, which makes sense since the three of them have been disappearing together for a good couple years—even before Dad died. But I see it differently now.

It's all about the way they look at Ravi.

I notice the tension in them right away during Sunday lunch because the whispers stop when me and Columbus come into the room. It's always like that with Ma, Pammy and Aunty K. They're usually really chatty when they're together, but they don't like to include anyone else. Behind us is Ravi, who doesn't seem to realize how weird this is for everyone but him. Even Columbus notices and he's usually unaware of anything but the food on the table at times like this.

Let's get out of here, he texts. *They're freaking me out.*

And get my ass whooped? I reply.

He makes some excuse about homework and bails before lunch. I don't think Pammy even notices. I should have gone with him, but there's something about Ma that scares me. There's silence around the table as we eat macaroni pie and callaloo with crab. Ravi's oblivious. Nobody says anything about how he's sitting in my dad's chair. Maybe it's not much of a difference to them, but it's huge for me.

Now I get it.

It's not the quiet, so much. It's not even that they all look completely burnt out. Dark circles under every set of eyes and gray hair showing on everyone's roots. It's the looks directed toward Ravi when he's not looking. He talks to Ma, but Pammy and Aunty K are staring only at him. He turns to ask me to pass the pepper sauce and all three of them zero in with their eerie looks, saying things to each other with them that Ravi and I aren't a part of.

Difference is, I know it's happening.

I've never met anyone more oblivious than Ravi, and I train at a Muay Thai gym where fighters can lose a brain cell or three hundred after a while.

Ravi squeezes Ma's ass while she clears the dishes from the table. I think I throw up in my mouth a little. Wait, a lot.

Her smile has a hard edge to it, which he also doesn't notice. He's only eaten half of what's on his plate and seems weaker for it. He's lost weight and not in any of the good areas. The muscles in his arms are withering and I bet I can lift more than him now. He wanders into the living room and changes the channel on the TV to cricket, which is barely a sport.

Ma takes his plate away. The three of them, Ma, Pammy, Aunty K, seem satisfied somehow.

I can't stand it. The looks!

Like they know things, secret things. Female things. And I'm back to the day of Dad's funeral, when they were all in this kitchen, looking at each other. Something passing between them. I'm frightened but I can't seem to move either. I want some of what Columbus has, that boy obliviousness I've never had the luxury of losing myself to.

I want the gym, too, but it's closed. The last time I was there, I took Dad's phone from the locker and put it back into my bag. Now I wish I'd just left it there. I don't even know what to do with it, to be honest.

I go upstairs and strip down to my underwear and start to

shadowbox in the mirror. The food I just ate threatens to come back up, but I will it to settle because I need my strength. After twenty minutes, I'm covered in sweat and bored of moving around this tiny rectangular room, so I drop and do push-ups until I see stars.

Somewhere after the stars, there's a face.

At first, I think it's the girl, whoever it is, that I'm going to fight in Florida my first round. Her hair is cut short to her scalp . . . then I realize it isn't a girl at all.

The face that comes into focus is male, tired, drawn. Shocked. It's Dad, split lip visible as he turns. Lit up by a dim streetlight in the middle of a rainy night, his body half toward us, stumbling back, like he'd been propelled forward somehow, pushed even, and was just realizing that we were almost upon him.

His eyes that won't close, until they do.

For the last time.

My scream.

Pammy throwing her arms around me, sobbing that he's with the angels now, that it's not my fault. Not my fault. A shadow sliding along the parking lot, and into the trees.

Ma wrapping her arm around me, sobbing now too: "She didn't *murder* him. He came out at us. He was drunk! It was raining!"

Is raining, I remember thinking. *It is raining, still.*

But she'd already made the story up in her head and that's how she was going to tell it. The night was dark, he was drunk and it was raining. Ma couldn't have known he was drunk at the time, except she knew that he drank a lot and that he probably was. And she was right, in the end. That's why they didn't take away my learner's permit. There'd been so much booze in his system and I didn't mean to murder my own father. Why would I?

But I can't stop thinking about the lock that Ravi said he broke, and the fact that Dad had a bloody lip even before the accident. Was Ravi there that night? Did something happen between him and Dad?

I'm hoping a hot shower will help me forget, and as I stand under the stream of water, I stop thinking. After the water turns cold, I go downstairs for a drink and see that, within an hour and a half of leaving the table, Ravi is asleep on the couch.

In the middle of the afternoon.

Ma's purse is on the table. There's money in it—there's always money in it these days, but I reach for her car keys. The glove compartment in the car was the last place I saw the key to the safe deposit box. Nobody notices as I slip downstairs to her car. It's freezing outside, so I don't linger. They don't notice, either, when I come in again.

twenty

At the bank, Columbus is impatient. "What are we doing here?"

"Just wait." I leave him in the car, and I show the key to the woman at reception. She leads me down the hall to the room with all the safe deposit boxes. I'm sweating in my giant yellow parka, even though it's cold in here and cold outside.

The woman notices. "You alright, honey?"

"I'm eighteen," I say, again. I wipe my hands on my jeans, but she doesn't notice.

"I know. You showed me your passport."

"Right. Yeah."

We both put our keys into the double lock of Box 4242, and she slides the box out for me. It's smaller than I expected. She puts it on a desk in the corner and turns away to give me some privacy. But she doesn't leave the room. Everything from the lockbox is in there, plus some papers I've never seen before. I slip the papers into my bag. The woman leads me back out, all calm like, and I'm acting so wrong, so suspicious, that I figure she must be bored with her job or something to let all this slide. My eyes are darting everywhere and I can't even get a sentence out. I think she's going to give a signal to the security guard to snatch me when I'm about to leave, but I walk out the door just fine. Like nothing ever happened. When I do look back, though, she's watching me. In no time at all I'm back in the car.

"Let's get out of here," I say to Columbus.

We go to the beaches by Woodbine Avenue. He's not happy because I said we'd go for KFC, and I flat out lied about that. We park, but don't get out of the car. The grass, the sand, the walkways are covered in snow and ice. The wind by the lake is something fierce, kicking up the water. It's too cold to go outside so we sit in the car with the engine turned on for heat while we go through the papers. I don't want to do it alone. If Ma can pull Pammy into whatever storm she's got brewing, then I can have Columbus. He's not much, but he's the best I've got.

He says something dumb about how bushy my hair is, but I just ignore it. He's in a mood due to the lack of KFC, and I wonder for the first time in ages how things are going with his mall retail worker.

All his lame jokes disappear as he reads over my shoulder.

"Three years ago," he says, frowning, "your mom took out life insurance on your dad for a hundred thousand dollars?" He looks at me. "You guys have a hundred thousand dollars?"

He can hardly believe it, and neither can I. Three years. She got an insurance policy three years ago.

Maybe it's nothing, but if it's so nothing then why did she hide it from me but tell Pammy? "I don't know. Maybe it takes them a while to pay the money or something. Maybe they have to investigate to make sure you didn't murder the guy."

Columbus is on his phone now. "Okay, says here that if you have the policy for two years, you just get the dough. Almost no questions asked. It's not even worth the effort for the insurance company to pursue it unless it's millions of dollars."

"What are you looking at?"

"Online forum. Hey," he says, "didn't your dad have an accident in Trinidad last year? Someone attacked him?"

Columbus is a lot of things, but stupid isn't one of them. I wasn't going to bring it up, because it looks so bad and I've never been this confused in my life. "Kidnapping."

"What? Sorry, I didn't hear you."

I clear my throat and try again. "He thought someone tried to kidnap him. At his garage."

"He thought or someone did?"

I shake my head. It's anyone's guess.

"But that's weird, right? At the two-year mark, he's attacked?"

"It's Trinidad," I say. "Shit like that happens all the time."

He reads some more on his phone. "Says here that if someone is murdered then you can't get the money. Maybe your mom had a feeling something bad was going to happen or—"

I see the exact moment he gets it. That it could have been more than a bad feeling or some kind of mystical premonition crap. That she could have wanted something bad to happen.

Made it happen.

"Shit," he says, looking pale and scared.

"Don't tell anyone about this, okay? About this insurance stuff. Please?"

"Who would I tell?"

"Just don't mention it to Pammy."

He's confused. "Why? What does my mom have to do with any of this?"

"Just promise me. Please, Christopher?"

Two pleases in a row and his real name. This is unheard of for me. I never ask him for anything and I haven't called him Christopher since the first day I met him, ten years ago, when he and Pammy moved next door to us.

"Okay," he says. He must think he has something on me now, because he leans over and kisses me. His lips are dry, but it's not a bad kiss. I let him for a minute, until it becomes almost clear I'm not kissing him back. Maybe on a different day, I would have but I'm too shook by what I've just read.

Plus, it's not like kissing Jason at all.

It reminds me of how much I actually liked kissing Jason, who I don't really want to be thinking about right now because he hasn't called in a while. Hasn't even come to the gym. We texted a few times, but he only says he's busy with school and first year is even tougher than he thought it was going to be. I feel stupid, but I push it aside. Everyone knows this is why you don't date college guys when you're still in high school.

Columbus is the one to pull away. I guess he must feel how distracted I am. "Sorry." He gives me a too-bright smile.

We share a joint because we need something to help us get over that moment and it works because, after a minute, I can tell he really is sorry he kissed me. I make him drive me to a copy center and then back to the bank. We go slow and the both of us grow increasingly paranoid, but for different reasons. There's someone else at reception, a man this time. He checks something on the computer and says, "You were just here."

"Yeah, I forgot something."

He takes a long look at me and I can tell he's thinking, *This is weird and she's maybe high,* but there's nothing he can do because it's my box. I put the insurance papers back where I found them and get out of there as quickly as I can. The man watches me the whole time.

That night, Ma comes into my room and wakes me. "I got a message from the bank today, checking to see if we're happy with their services. You went into the safe deposit box? Why? Where's the key?"

"Ma, I'm sleeping," I say, pulling the covers back over my head.

But it's like she knows. I know that she knows that I know about the insurance papers. I feel her looking at me in the dark. Her eyes, when I see them just for a second, are like flint, like ancient pieces of stone all sharp and hard. Her hair smells like coconuts, like the oil she uses to condition it, but there's an odd, musty scent underneath it. Like an old skin that she's just pulled back onto herself. Her hands, when they pause on my bare arm, are rough. There's a bruise just above my elbow. Her fingers linger on it, for just a second. Somehow she must sense the skin there is fragile. I think she's going to press on it, and my whole body tenses in anticipation of a pain that never comes.

There's a pause that seems to go on forever and I'm about to tell her everything, but then I feel her move away. "We'll talk about this tomorrow."

I hear her walking about afterwards, hear her in the shower, washing her old skin. I hear muttering.

A voice that comes out at me in the darkness.

Just when the house quiets, a blast of steel pan blares out. I tumble to the floor and reach into my gym bag to turn the phone off. It trembles in my hand, falls onto the carpet, and I hear footsteps coming down the hall toward me. The song stops just a split second before the footsteps pause outside of my door. I lay there on the ground, not daring to move or breathe, not even to shove the phone back into the bag or under the bed. If she comes in now, I'm dead.

In the dark, on the floor, I press my hands over my mouth and think: *I'm dead I'm dead I'm dead I'm dead I'm dead I'm dead I'm dead I'm dead . . .*

Not yet, says a voice in my head, clear and sharp. *But you can be.*

The footsteps move away—

What was it she always said to me? *I brought you into this world, and I can take you out of it.*

—but for now, she's gone.

Hands shaking, I pick up the phone and dial the last number that called. "Hello?" says a quiet male voice on the other side.

"It's me. Trisha. Can we talk?"

"That's why I'm calling," says Junior. My brother. It doesn't seem so strange, after all, to think that I have a brother out there in the world.

twenty-one

When Ma was younger, she went to work as a domestic for a young family in Trinidad. There are photos in Aunty K's album of what she looked like back then. In case you're wondering, she was a dime. Seventeen years old, just a year younger than me.

The affair with the man of the house was no surprise to anybody. He was just married, and his pregnant bride was the size of a planet. He was no good, had never been any good, and didn't plan on absorbing any goodness around him anytime soon. Of course he was going to stay with his wife because that shit still matters in Trinidad, no mind that he knocked up the maid. That's just the kind of dude he was, my father. Sent her to Canada to live with some of her relatives. Gave her some money for school. By the time her sister, who was living in New York, heard about the whole thing, Ma was already six months preggers with me and enrolled in nursing courses.

Ma used all her stupidity up on one thing: my dad. And she let it use her up for over eighteen years. Let him come and go as he pleased. He paid for her schooling, which she hid from Aunty K. She thought he'd leave his wife for her, and fat chance of that.

The baby his wife had? Was a boy.

And the maid's baby isn't any reason for someone to leave their son and their wife they married in a proper(ish) Hindu ceremony, the one where the woman dresses in a red sari and walks with her groom around the fire. But a pretty, poor servant like Ma and a daughter like me? He didn't even come up to meet me when I was born. In the baby photos it's just Aunty K, Ma and me. And later, Pammy and Columbus. That's my family.

This brother, now. Junior. I've never met him before, but I know he's around my age. We've been talking. I've known about him my whole life, but Dad always kept us apart. I think Ma wanted him to. I'm trying to work up the courage to ask what I really want to ask about Dad in Trinidad. But I'm distracted. It's all so new. We talk every night for a week. About school, mostly. I tell him about Muay Thai, but he can't get it straight from MMA. "So there's no cage?" he says, sounding kind of disappointed. He's not even a year older than me.

I send him some videos, and a clip from my last fight. It takes him a long time to respond. "You look like Dad."

The way he says it confuses me, like we shared him or something. Like he belonged to the both of us. This had never occurred to me, before, but I guess that's what you'd think, maybe, if you didn't know what it was like in that co-op townhouse me and Ma share, and sometimes shared with him. That we'd been a family of a kind, and that he'd been a big part of it, or had an equal third. That some part of him belonged to me as much as it did to my brother I've never laid eyes on. I don't have any pictures of Dad handy, but I have an image of him in my memory, so I dredge it up and hold it in my mind. I look closer at the video but I don't see it, this resemblance that my brother believes is there. I don't look like Dad at all. I don't look like anybody.

But what Junior said gets me thinking about Dad. Then I start on the service after the cremation, and the moment in the kitchen just after Ma, Aunty K and Pammy looked at each other in that strange way.

I make myself remember that it wasn't just the look that bothered me. There was a banging at the door and a woman downstairs, a polite young man next to her. The woman's hair was wild, flying everywhere, and she wasn't dressed for a Toronto fall. She looked like she'd just stepped off a plane. Neither of them was wearing a jacket. I saw them from the kitchen window. Saw Aunty K go down to speak to them. I opened the window, but I couldn't hear anything Aunty K was saying, only that whatever it was, she was mad as hell. Ma went out and approached the woman, but Pammy pulled her back. Seeing Ma shocked the woman, who stumbled back into her son's arms.

Her son, my brother, Junior.

This moment, so fresh in my mind. The woman was talking, blubbering, and I thought she was saying to Ma "You kill him?" over and over.

I was so sure it was a question but now . . . now, I'm not.

twenty-two

Against an indigo backdrop, Noor's got her guard up. It looks like she's standing against the night, like she's part of it and it's part of her. She's sporting brand new leggings under her Thai shorts and a long-sleeve top that covers her from neck to wrist. She shadowboxes for a few seconds and then turns to the camera and says her name, a bit about her journey to becoming a fighter and what the Florida tournament means to her.

The camera guy asks her if her family's traditional and what they think of her fighting. What that means in a cultural context.

She slaps him with a glare so gangster he takes a step back. Kru tries to hide a grin, badly. With Noor, like with me, family is a no-fly zone. When she steps down from the little platform in the lobby she rolls her eyes at me and I roll mine right back. As with discussions about who's more likely to be a ho based on skin color, there's no space for conversations about family and traditions here.

Amanda's next and she pretty much does the same thing as Noor, only she's wearing a sports bra and her shorts, wraps and ankle sleeves. In her little video spiel, she just says her name and, with a fierce frown, challenges the camera guy to ask for more. He's learned his lesson, though, and just thanks her.

Kru gives her an exasperated look, but doesn't push her to say anything else. When I get up there, the camera guy sighs heavily. He's clearly over the novelty of doing promo shots for female fighters. He runs a hand over the springy hairs threatening to escape from the top of his T-shirt. "Take your mouth guard out, please."

I do, but I have nowhere to put it so I hold it since I'm just wearing wraps. Kru gives me a shooing motion, which I take to mean "do something" even though what he's indicating is the exact opposite. It's a lot harder than it looks, mugging for the camera, so I start to shadowbox.

"Turn more to the camera . . . oh, Jesus. Don't look like someone just murdered your family."

There's a moment of horrified silence. "What?" says the camera guy.

Amanda and Noor are looking like they want to murder *him*, but Kru clearly wants to get on with the day. "Give her a minute," Kru says.

The camera guy frowns. "I've got another job right after this."

I catch a glimpse of myself in the small mirror over the reception desk. Who is this girl, with her hair coiled into a neat braid? Even more important, who does she think she is? Not a fighter, that's for sure! Look at her technique. Look at how she can't even say her name for the camera. How she pulls faces, trying to convince the lens that she's stronger than she is. Okay, so maybe there's been a murder in her family, but is that really an excuse here?

She doesn't look like a fighter to me, this girl.

Also, she isn't really a girl anymore. I mean, she isn't young. She's old enough to know better, be better. Her guard keeps dropping. She taunts me with her lack of ability to do even this simple thing. Pretend for the camera—how difficult is that?

No matter how hard I try, I can't get it right until Kru takes me aside and says, "Think of something that makes you feel like you're on top of the world. That makes you feel powerful. Or made you feel that way once, even just for a moment. You got something like that?"

I nod. My right hand is oddly numb, until I realize it's wrapped around my mouth guard. So I loosen it up, scratch at an itch I've got on my neck, and think about the night Dad died. I guess the talk about murder in my family gives me what I need, some kind of fierceness. I put my guard up and tuck my chin in.

"Better than nothing," says the camera guy.

"Whatever you're thinking, that's what you need to take with you into the ring," Kru says while the camera guy packs his gear. He pats me on the back. "We're going to put these photos and the videos up in the next couple weeks, right after your school break, to get people excited for the fighters going to Florida."

That's what I like about Kru. He could have said "girls," or even the more generic, genderless "guys." He could have said "young ladies." He could have said any other thing but he calls us the thing that we want to be, even if we might not be quite there yet. He calls us fighters, and that's just about the best option. It's enough to make me forget, for a long spell afterwards, that I look like there's been a murder in my family. That despite all my attempts to push it down, bury it deep, I've been wearing it on my face all this time. In plain view, for everyone to see.

I remember the exact passage where I stopped reading the soucouyant book that I gave back to Mr. Abdi.

"Your history is a living book . . . Your history is your grammar for life . . ."

My history is a travel guidebook. My history is a creature nobody really believes in. My history is a foreign word.

My history is so fucked up, I wouldn't even know where to start.

twenty-three

I'm looking forward to New York for March Break next week. I definitely don't want to stay here with Ma and Ravi. I say so to Junior, up in my bedroom. We're on video chat, which we've started to do. It's pretty late but Ma is at work and I don't know where Ravi is, so it feels safe to talk to him.

He's wearing a bright blue T-shirt and a pair of gold-rimmed glasses. He looks so much like Dad, way more than me. I don't know what he was talking about with my fight video.

Junior and his uncle on his mom's side run Dad's garage now, in Trinidad. After a while of talking about that and his plans to go to university in the fall, I ask Junior about the time about a year ago when Dad was attacked.

"Everyone was gone from the garage for the night and Dad was just coming out from upstairs—"

"Upstairs?"

"Yeah, there's an apartment above the garage."

"So he was on the second floor?" I hadn't heard that part. I thought he was attacked right outside the garage.

"Yeah. The man was trying to drag him down the stairs to the car, but Dad had a wrench on him and got in a few knocks. Still, he said he almost fell down those concrete steps and broke his neck. We went to the hospital with him, me and Mom. The man busted up his eye real good, but he wasn't getting in nobody's car. They kidnap you like that down here, get your family to pay the money to get you back. Sometimes they pay the money and you don't come back."

"So he was at the top of the stairs when he was attacked? Why didn't the attacker wait until he got down the stairs?"

Junior shakes his head. "I don't know."

"What did Dad say about it?"

"He didn't say anything. But he was real careful after that. He thought they would go after me or Mommy next, but they never did. Everybody knows everybody in this place. It's hard if you not from around here to get away with anything. Only time anybody free up is at Carnival."

It doesn't make sense that someone would try to attack him from the top of the stairs, right? Not when you could fall so easily. I don't want to think this, I really don't, but what if that was the whole reason for the attack? Columbus said that you wouldn't get the insurance money if someone died during a murder. But you would if it was an accident.

Like a fall down some concrete steps.

I'm so lost in thought that it takes me a moment to

realize that Junior is still talking about Carnival, about J'ouvert last year and how much fun it was. "If you want to come back for Carnival next year, I'll take you. My friends have a band, so we can get a costume and everything for you if you want. You ever play Mas in Toronto?"

Me, play masquerade in bright, bejewelled underwear? There's a Caribbean festival in Toronto every summer, but you'll never catch me there. I shake my head, but I say I'll think about it anyway.

Then something unexpected happens.

His mother comes in. Junior doesn't look embarrassed or hide or anything. He turns the screen toward her so that she can see me. "Is that Trisha?" she asks.

I wave at her. She looks so different from that time she came to the house after Dad's funeral, when her hair was all wild and she looked like she was going mad with grief. Now, she seems . . . really, really nice. She's got this kind, open face. I can almost read every thought on it. If you've ever summoned up an image of a perfect wife from Trinidad, she would be it.

Right now, Dad's perfect wife is staring at my neck. "Soucouyant biting you," she says.

"What?"

"Soucouyant come at night, you know? Shed she skin, turn into a vampire and bite people." She points to my throat, where the base of my neck meets my collarbone. There are some scratches there that have scarred in a way that almost look like freckles. One of them is even fresh.

I don't remember how I got these scratches but they must have been from training. "But that's . . . that's a story."

"Ma, stop it," Junior says. He grins and it's like watching Dad. That's why they call him Junior, I guess. He's a little Dad, everyone's pride and joy. That smile and the way his eyes crinkle when he does it. Dad didn't smile like that often toward the end because he and Mom were complicated. But seeing how happy my brother is, how sweet his mom seems . . . I wonder why Dad ever came up here to mess with me and Ma.

If he hadn't, he'd still be alive.

Junior's mom waves goodbye to me and leaves the room. Junior is still smiling. "You know what you have to do now, right?"

I pull up the neck of my hoodie a little and try to hide the marks. Maybe I got them clinching? "What?"

"You have to put a line of salt down by your door so the soucouyant has to stop and count each grain. Then she can't get back to her skin before the morning comes and she dies."

"I heard you have to find the skin and put it in salt." Did I read that in the soucouyant book or did I hear it in the roti shop?

"What? No. Trust me, I'm an expert." He says it in this braggadocious way, but I can tell he's joking. It's another

154

part of my brother that I file away. How easily he laughs and jokes around.

"Your mom seems nice."

He gets shy all of a sudden. "Yeah, she alright."

"I'm sorry," I say. "About Dad. And how you couldn't come to the service."

"We didn't find out until the day before. Man had two families. Nothing to be sorry about, really. Ma had a prayers for him here. I tried to call the phone to invite you, but it was turned off."

Hindu prayers after someone's death isn't the same as a funeral, giving last rites to a body. It should have been here, for him. He should have been in Trinidad with these people who lived with him and loved him, instead of in Toronto with me and Ma. What was he doing with us, anyway, when he had Junior and his wife back home? It must have been some voodoo Ma put on him. Whether she wanted to or not.

"You gonna come and visit, right?"

I lift my shoulder and let it fall back. "I don't know."

"I understand," says Junior, this new brother of mine. "Trinidad ain't for everybody. When was the last time you came home?"

"When I was a kid. I barely remember it at all. It just felt that I didn't belong there."

He laughs. "You don't have to belong to visit your brother."

Now I'm laughing, too, even though I don't know why. There's something easy there, an easiness of the people, of life—

When you're not busy getting kidnapped for ransom or murdered by gangsters or worn straight down to the bone by corrupt politicians.

—but it's not mine. Easy doesn't suit me particularly well, I don't think. But I laugh with him anyway because he's my brother and, right now, maybe I don't feel so alone.

Junior goes quiet for a moment. "Can I ask you something?"

"Yeah."

"What really happened that night?"

I know which night he's talking about, but I still say it. "The night Dad died? It was raining. And the car . . ."

And I hear something. Something I shouldn't. A footstep at the door.

I look up and see Ma's face, staring at me from the hallway. She's shocked. More than that, she's angry. I don't think I've ever seen her so mad. She turns and leaves, her footsteps padding down the stairs. I don't hear them like I usually do because somehow, somewhere, she learned how to sneak around a lot better.

And I'm scared, because she wasn't supposed to hear me on the phone, talking about Dad.

Especially not talking to my brother about him.

twenty-four

Because I'm a coward and I don't want to face Ma yet, I run a bath and pour some Epsom salt in to help with my sore muscles. Then look at the bag of salt and remember what Junior said. It sounds insane. If I was a mythical demon creature, I'd try to have a less common weakness. Like something you can't buy at any grocery store, maybe?

Eventually, after my bath, I work up the courage to go downstairs. Ma's on her hands and knees on the kitchen floor, scrubbing the corner of the room. When she sees me in the doorway, she gets to her feet and pulls the latex gloves from her hands. "Come here."

Like a zombie, I do. I stand in front of her with my hands curled into fists.

"Who were you talking to?" she says, her voice so quiet I almost want to lean in to hear her better. But even I know this is a bad idea.

"A friend." I make this sound as breezy as I can, but I can tell right away that I'm in more trouble than I'd thought. And I'd thought I was in a lot.

She gives me the look. You know. *The look*. She comes

toward me. Fighting the urge to glance at the dent on the wall, I just back into the hallway . . .

But she blocks the stairwell going up the stairs before I can get to it.

"What friend were you talking to about the night your father died?"

"Someone from school." I try to move past her, but she grabs my arm.

"You feel I'm stupid or what? I heard the voice! Who's the boy?"

"Nobody!"

"You want to play woman? Well, go be woman then. Go be woman in your own house!" When she's mad like this her accent gets thick and her voice is rapid-fire. I can barely keep up. "All this time I think you was in school and going to that gym, and now I find out you have some boy you keeping from me? Talking about things you have no place to be saying? Telling people our business? You been whoring about this town, Trisha?" And then, even worse, because she's gone this far and isn't backing down: "Me, raise a *jamette*?"

I don't know how to explain what it's like when your own mother calls you a skank, but I'm suddenly a little girl again with hot, bitter tears washing my face.

"You're one to talk! You and Dad weren't even married!" I try to wrench my arm away, but she's too angry to be shaken off. She hangs on for dear life. Mine and hers.

"You know what it was like when I met your father! You saw what happened to me . . . why would you . . . Tell me, who is he? Who's this friend?"

So I'm the one to blame for her shitty life? I think of Junior's mom, with her sweet round face and her nice smile. Why couldn't she be my mother? "Let go of me!" I could push her off, but I don't want to hurt her. I know I'm stronger than I look. But, I guess, so is she.

"What's his name, Trisha?"

And now I'm so mad. It's like something's burst inside me, so I tell her. "Junior. His name is Junior, and he's my brother."

She reels, as though from a blow. If I were to hit her, though, she'd be on the floor. I know that one hundred percent. *One hundred percent.*

"Your brother," she whispers.

"And his mom, too. Remember you saw her? She came to our house the day of the funeral. And Aunty K sent her away."

She goes silent at the mention of Junior's name, but her nails still grip my arm. I think I'm bleeding, but I don't tear my eyes away to check.

Ma looks scared, and I guess that makes me bold. Makes me reckless.

"Junior saw Ravi, Ma. Back last year when Dad got attacked. He was there and he saw Ravi on the stairs. And

Columbus saw Ravi, too. The night Dad died. Ravi was trying to break into the house when he knew me, you and Aunty K were gone and only Dad would be there."

I'm sure she can tell I'm lying, she's looking right at me, but something has come over her. She becomes someone that's not my ma. Someone I don't even recognize. Her hair is wild about her face and she bares her sharp teeth and exhales a stream of hot, sickly sweet breath that's oddly metallic. Like there's blood in her mouth.

I'm not sure if it's an accident, what happens next.

All I know is that I pull away and she goes with me, with force. Either the wall or the landing breaks my fall, I don't know, but my arm twists under me and the pain is like nothing I've ever felt before. I look up at her stark face and it's not until I feel the tears drip off my chin and onto the floor that I realize we're both crying.

For me it's not sadness, it's shock.

I can't seem to move anything without feeling like I'm being stabbed on my left side.

Then she's next to me, pulling me to her. Her soft arms are around me and she whispers "my baby" over and over. "You don't know," she says. "You don't know what I sacrificed for you. My baby." Her kisses fall on my face, my hair, my closed eyes. There's a plinging in my head, like a steel pan. I think I hear her whisper "forgive me" but I'm not sure. The steel pan gets louder, filling my ears with a drum beat that falls in tune with my heart.

My baby

Forgive me

You're mine

Jamette

You're mine

There's a spot of blood on my cheek. I must have scraped it when I fell. She's staring at it, then she licks her dry lips. She lets me go, turns nurse-like. "You smell like salt."

From our tears? From the Epsom salt in my bath?

I watch her as she goes about examining my arm, running her hands along my body to check for other injuries. All business, all work now. "Let's get you to the ER."

She helps me to my feet and keeps her hand on my back to guide me to the door. There's a cold efficiency to it, a separation of what came before. I remember this is what it was like with my dad, after. After the bruising, the hitting, comes this practicality. Let's mend now. Let's take care of you. Wipe away your blood, your tears, and tell you how beautiful you are, how you're the best thing that ever happened to me, to us, to these shitty lives of ours that we live in this country that is freezing for most of the year and sunk in unbearable heat when the snow melts.

But what she's really saying, what he was, is that you're mine.

You're mine.

twenty-five

We were told that there's no operative treatment for an acromioclavicular joint separation and all I can do is wear a sling and take it easy. But my whole arm is useless, itchy under the sling, and I'm completely and totally fucked for the gym now. As soon as I can take pressure on it again, I have to be training to make weight for Florida, which is in less than two months. No reprieve on the school end, either. Because of the injury Ma wouldn't let me go to New York for March Break, so I was stuck in the house with her and Ravi the whole time, which is what I'd been trying to avoid.

You have no idea how glad I was when school started up again.

The one benefit of this whole thing is that I can text just fine with my left hand, something Jason and I discovered when someone from the gym told him about my accident and he blew up my phone asking me what happened. Obviously I couldn't tell him, because snitches get acromioclavicular joint separations, but it was sweet.

He's sweet.

Jason meets me at Kennedy station after class almost every day for a week. He's a freshman at the University of Toronto's downtown campus. Doing political science? Something like that.

"Girl, he's in love with you," says Noor, when Jason leaves on his train going west. It's one of the rare days when The Fiancé isn't around to pick her up, so she and Amanda have decided to meet up to harass me. Because they're here, Jason didn't kiss me goodbye like he usually does, so I'm a little pissed at them right now for existing. We're really getting the hang of it now, Jason and me. Every time feels even better than the last, and I try not to wonder if he's practising with the college girls he's probably swimming in. Ones who don't know his abs are just for show. I don't even mind anymore that his muscles are mostly decorative, so why would they?

Speaking of muscles. Today I tried to do some weights but Kru wouldn't let me. He said it was important to "heal" or something. He saw how disappointed I was and tried to pat my shoulder in commiseration, but I wasn't really having any of it today. I sat in the corner playing chess with a twelve-year-old who was better than me until everyone was done.

"You fell down the stairs? What an old-lady way to hurt your arm," says Amanda. She's training hard for Florida, harder than the rest of us. I'm pretty jealous and, I think, so is Noor. Amanda's been killing it and she's even got her videos on the gym social media almost every day. You either want to be her or fight her, and in my current shape, I wouldn't want to fight her. In my best shape I wouldn't want to fight her. Or Noor, or Imelda. There's too much respect. I want nothing more than to spar with them again but I can't right now and my arm hurts too much for me to even remember why I got hurt in the first place.

The how I remember, but the why is a mystery.

At home, I see Ma has been cooking up a storm. Dhalpuri, curry channa and aloo, baigan choka. I dunno, I think she forgot I can only eat with one hand right now and curry maybe isn't the best thing to give someone who's gotta be mindful of a bum limb, but I don't bring it up because we're not really talking. When she notices what she's done, she kisses her teeth in that Caribbean way that tells you every-thing about her mood and takes my plate away to put everything in the roti and fold it up nice and tight. Then she turns her back and I can hear her crying at the sink.

She hasn't been able to look at me since it happened, so she looks around me. Near me. I don't know what to say to her either. She makes sure I take my vitamins and my pain-killers but watches me real careful when I do.

Ravi . . . well, who knows what to think about Ravi. He's the one who drove us home from the hospital because I guess Ma hadn't wanted to be alone with me in the car—

So Ravi is somehow the peacemaker? Fuckkkkk that.

—but he keeps disappearing because it seems to get too hot up in the house these days. He does make sure to eat before he goes, because why pass up a good thing?

He looks different, though. Like, I don't even know what to say. He falls asleep all the time and when he's looking at you sometimes, it's like his pupils are huge in his eye sockets. Huge, dark pits that seem to be keeping something trapped. Every now and then he slurs his speech, like Dad when he was drunk. Except Ravi doesn't drink, not really. I hardly ever see him crack a beer. So he must be getting faded on something else, which of course makes me think of those vials under the sink and the pills I found in his bag.

I message Columbus to see what he's up to. He doesn't respond. I think maybe he has a new girlfriend or something. Or his mall girl is back in his life. I finish some reading for World Issues, then I see two messages waiting for me. From Jason.

I wish your friends weren't there today.

We missed our goodbye.

He means the little make-out sessions we've been having. I send him a kiss emoji and he sends me one back. Then a minute later my phone lights up with another text from him.

Want to come over?

I drop the phone. What does a panic attack feel like? I think I'm having a panic attack.

I ask Columbus for advice. He sends an eggplant emoji. So do Noor and Amanda.

I need to get new friends.

Jason texts again. ???

Noor asks if I want to go, if I'm ready for that step. She knows you don't go hang out at a guy's place UNLESS.

I think about it for a moment, if I really do want to see Jason tonight. We did miss our goodbye. I mean, I did. I missed it, too. Maybe it's not too late to have one. Could be the bad arm is doing something to my head because I can't stop thinking about what happens next.

He lives in residence at U of T. I have butterflies, like they say in those books I used to read when I was thirteen years old. With the rich and handsome duke or whatever, who would sweep some chimney maid into his arms and then (afterwards) discover that she was some other duke's bastard daughter. But duke spunk is potent as fuck and makes everything okay, so it always turned out fine in the end.

Anyway, I'm here with Jason in his dorm room and I can't stop looking at him. He's got dark hair and eyes, but his skin is kind of pale. Even though it's perfect and unblemished, I wonder when was the last time he was in Mexico and got any sun. And I wonder, too, if he got into a school like this and is living in res, who the hell is he and what's he doing at my gym in Scarborough?

But I don't ask him about any of that. We talk about books. I tell him about Mr. Abdi being disappointed in my *Gatsby* essay, but there was nothing he could do about it. The term was over. So he just gave me an A, as per usual, and wrote me off, probably.

"But you're doing business management next year?" Jason says.

"Yeah, I kind of have to."

"Why do you have to?"

I shrug. "Because I'm not going to be a doctor." Which is the Caribbean expectation. If you're not a doctor, you're a banker. So I've got to get that business or finance degree before I apply to banks because that's the way it works.

"I get it," he says. "I wanted to go to film school but my parents thought it would be nice to have a poli sci background. They think I could get a government job."

All immigrant kids know that a government job is not as good as becoming a doctor, but it's definitely as good as a banker so it's still up there. I could see Jason doing it, too. But it doesn't seem to be what he wants. He doesn't sound bitter about this at all, just a little sad. "What kind of films would you make?"

"Horror, but not the gory kind. The kind that's about what happens when real life goes wrong."

Ha. When real life goes wrong? I could tell him some stories.

"There's that look on your face," he says, putting a finger on my forehead.

"What look?"

"That one right there. Every time we talk about something other than the gym, you close up."

"No, I don't." I push his hand away.

"Yeah, you do. I asked about your dad last week, remember? I mean, he just died. I thought you'd want to talk about it. But you changed the subject."

He's right. "Because it's been a bit crazy at my house lately. I found out my mom took out an insurance policy on my dad." Damn. That just slipped out.

Jason sits back on his bed. "Is that weird?"

"Yeah, it is. She never told me she did, and then she tried to hide the information from me. Plus, she's got this new boyfriend, right after Dad dies. She won't even talk about how they met. It's like everything is a secret all of a sudden."

He goes quiet for a moment. "Sounds messed up."

I really don't want to talk about Dad anymore. But I like that Jason offered. Like I could talk if I wanted to—or was allowed to.

Jason is just there, across from me on his bed. I'm on the hard, narrow chair by his desk and noticing that he's one of those guys that gets better looking the longer you look at him. I want him to kiss me and I guess he wants it too because the second I uncross my legs, he leans forward. His lips are on mine and before I know it, I'm under him and on his bed.

We fool around for a while. I think I'm going to feel like it's enough soon, and I'll get up and go. But truthfully, I dead-ass don't get to the point where it's enough.

"You alright?" he asks. Both our shirts are off. He doesn't seem to mind that I'm wearing a regular sports bra. Whatevs, it's clean.

"Yeah." Still don't want to go.

"Do you want to stop?"

I don't even have to think about it. "No."

Jason knows it's my first time, so he's really careful. I watch in fascination as he puts on a condom. When he tries to kiss below my belly button, I clench my thighs together so he can't open me up, and I only relax when his mouth is back on mine. When he's inside me and I feel . . . I don't know where to start. I'm happy to feel him pressing against me.

I guess I never thought it was gonna be like this.

After.

The sex was okay, minus the O. Right away, almost immediately, he asked me if I came. I said yes, because he looked so eager. Then he fell asleep on top of me, so I wiggled out from under him, texted Noor and asked her what coming feels like. I probably could have waited but I felt like I needed to talk to someone. She said, *Psshhtt. You would know it when it happens. Where r u? Want me to get Hassan to pick u up?*

I'm good.

Jason wanted to tag along with me when I left, to at least see me partway home, but I was gone before he could get his clothes on. I kinda like riding the subway at night anyway. It's empty, quiet.

He didn't hurt you, did he? Noor manages to sound mad, even through a text.

No, I write back. It didn't hurt, really. Definitely not more than that time Amanda's elbow caught me on the chin and I went flying into the wall, which was even more painful than my acromioclavicular separation. But it didn't feel good either.

What feels good:

Jason's body on top of mine. Like clinching, but better. Less sweat, anyway. I liked putting my hands on his back and feeling the muscles there as he moved. That was maybe better than good.

A sense of closeness to him that I feel now.

This feeling now, that I'm no longer a virgin.

The knowledge that I've got something over Ma's head now.

Pammy's outside smoking when I get back. It's the middle of the night and she's in her lawn chair on her tiny porch, wrapped in a blanket, blowing smoke on long exhales. Even with all the smoking and periods of chain-smoking, her lung capacity is enormous, and this I know from the years of listening to her shout at Columbus.

She looks me up and down. Takes in my mussed hair and smudged mascara. Knows immediately what I've been up to, but it's Pammy and she doesn't really judge. "I hope you used protection, Trisha. Your sexual health is nothing to play around with. Did you have fun, at least?" she asks.

I don't answer. It was . . . I don't know yet. She seems to understand this.

"It can be like that sometimes. Hang on. I've got something for you." She grounds out her cigarette and disappears inside. Two minutes later she comes back out with a book. *"How to Find Your Bliss,"* she says, handing it to me. "A woman has to be responsible for her own orgasms."

"Oh." There's no hole in the ground to disappear into, but I still spend some time looking for one. I'm not sore, like I thought I might be, but I am tired.

She lights up another cigarette and gives me a small smile. "Just another thing you've got to take care of yourself. I keep telling my son, you have to help the woman find her pleasure, but not all mothers do that. Although they should. We women, we've got to look out for one another."

I get the feeling that she's not just talking about orgasms, but there's no way in hell I'm going to ask now.

"Can you not tell Ma about this?" I ask.

She stares at me for a moment, then lights another cigarette. "We all have secrets," she says.

What the hell does that mean? Is that a yes or a no? But Pammy closes her eyes and leans back in her chair and I don't feel like pushing her. She's either going to tell Ma or she isn't. Nothing I can do about it now.

I go inside and crawl into the shower. There's a bruise just below my ear that's turned red and I try to remember if Jason had put his mouth there. He must have. I press it until I feel the blood rushing back at me to meet my fingertip. There's that post-gym feeling now where all I want to do is sleep. The house is silent, which I take to mean Ma hasn't noticed I was gone. Good.

After the shower, I stand in front of the bathroom mirror and look from the bruise to my face as a whole. I think I see some kind of new knowledge in it. Not orgasmic knowledge, clearly. But it's something that marks me as a woman now. I've had dick and, even though it wasn't necessarily good in the way it's supposed to be (from the pictures in Pammy's book), it must mean something. But I don't know what.

twenty-six

Finally, I can take my sling off. My upper body strength is seriously gone, and I know I've got a lot of work to do to get it back. And my shoulder *hurts*. After the doctor's office, Ma drops me off at home while she goes to do some errands. I'm glad that she's not around to hover right now.

I text Jason as soon as I get inside to tell him I don't have a sling to worry about anymore, but he doesn't reply. I haven't heard from him for a few days, since the night at his dorm, really. He hasn't called. Or texted. Or showed any signs that he's alive.

See, this is why catching feelings is a bad idea.

Speaking of feelings, bad ones, Ravi is on the couch again. In the same spot he was in when I left yesterday. I can never look at that groove in the sofa again without thinking of him. The man-shaped impression that he slinks into, getting smaller and smaller with each passing day. At least he's got a shirt on—actually, it looks like he's wearing two—so there's that. He's awake, his gaze flicking briefly to me, then back to the television. I look at him while pretending that I'm not. I search for clues that he's the hitting kind and finally decide that he is, but not with Ma. Right now he'd be too slow to get a grip on her, anyway.

"You ever been to Diego Martin?" I ask.

"I was there last year." Then he blinks, as if to clear something from his eyes. Some kind of fog. "Why?"

"That's where my dad was from."

It's the second time I've brought Dad up in front of him. He tenses. "So what?"

"Nothing. Just . . . what were you doing there?"

He kisses his teeth like Ma, which is meant to put me in my place without actually having to think up the right words, and turns up the volume on the television, as if the sound of a cricket match could drown out the sound of my question.

When I come back into the living room an hour later, he looks at me like he's never seen me before. It's the dumb expression that gives me courage. "You figure out the answer to my question yet?"

He blinks some more, but this time it's like he's trying to figure out who I am. Sitting there on our couch as though I'm the intruder. Whoever this man is, he's not the Ravi who had the strength to knock a container of protein powder from my hand, to put his finger in my face and threaten me.

"Why did you break the lock on our back door, Ravi? Did you come here that night to try to hurt Dad?"

For a moment it seems like he's going to answer me, like I've somehow gotten past this thickness that's blurring his vision, but he's gripped by something that my questions can't even penetrate. His guilt seeps into the silence of the room.

Who was that shadow slipping into the trees the night Dad died?

Why did Ravi have Dad's phone in his bag? Did Dad drop it and he just picked it up?

Who attacked Dad in Trinidad?

(I hated him, so why can't I let him go?)

It's dark now, the night spilling in through our open window. I watch him as he falls deeper into whatever void he slips through, in a state that I know somehow is dreamless. A dreamless, gaping void that he gets lost to all the time now, for some reason. Maybe when the crates fell on him it made a hole inside him. Maybe that's why he doesn't bother to turn on lights, because he's alright with the darkness pulling itself over him, covering him, keeping him locked inside himself.

But it doesn't explain why I'm sitting in the dark across from him, in the brand new leather armchair Ma bought last week.

I can stay here forever.

I fall asleep and when I wake up, I feel a presence in the darkness. Standing just inside the living room, a body that's like a wisp, a ghost turning solid in almost unbearable increments.

Real, and frightening.

Long strands of hair falling down its back. Fingers opening and closing into fists. Nails sharp. The creature is looking at Ravi and I can feel the malevolence roll off it in waves of electricity. It's what jolted me awake, what holds me silent. This feeling of hatred.

But I'm not silent enough.

I must have made some sound, some loosening of breath, some shift of my body. The creature turns to me. My mother shines through its eyes. "Baby," it says, sounding like Ma but not really. The voice that comes at me in the dark is smooth like honey, the Trinidadian lilt like music, like rain on galvanized roofing, like a place that is at once far away and much too close. "Baby, what are you doing up?"

"Ma?" I croak. My throat is dust.

"I'm here, baby," she says, putting her hands on my shoulders, helping me to my feet. "Come, let's get you to bed."

She leads me up the stairs and into my bedroom. Her hands plucking at me, rough skin passing over mine. I'm so tired I'm almost asleep on my feet, so she tucks me in as though I'm a child again and I feel that maybe I am because I let her. I let her pull the blankets over me. I let her touch my forehead. I let her kiss me just above my eyebrow, my lids falling shut. Long fingers stroke down from my shoulders. This is what possession is . . . "Your poor arm, my girl. My little girl. Do you want something for the pain?"

I hear her voice, but it's far away. I'm sliding through the darkness. Even though I can't acknowledge it, I do hear her say it, the way she has said to Ravi countless times since he's been here. *Do you want something for the pain?*

But I don't need it, whatever it is. I'm already in the void.

twenty-seven

I'm back at the gym two days after I take my sling off. I'm surprised I waited this long. My left side is weak, so I need to start building it back up if I'm going to be in shape for Florida. It's just over a month away. I'm hitting the heavy bag, working my swing kicks. Fifty on each side. Then push kicks—same. Grab the back of the bag and start skip knees, with my face pressed against the leather, whispering *you kill him* over and over, but it's not a question. And then *I'm dead*.

Jason comes in and lingers by the speed bag.

I haven't seen him since that night. Amanda's not here, but Imelda and Noor are.

Imelda doesn't know about Jason and me, but she sees Noor come over, sees her looking at him looking at me and calls me over. "Wanna hold pads for me?" she asks, even though I'm covered in sweat and my arms are shaking.

Jason looks like he's about to say something, but I turn my back to him and grab a pair of mitts from the wall. Imelda doesn't hit hard, but she's freaking precise. Every hit I take, I feel the impact up through my forearms, all the way to my shoulders. We do a couple rounds and I can barely move my arms. I sit on a bench in the ladies' locker room for a long time.

Noor puts her hand on my shoulder before she leaves. "He didn't call? No text, nothing?"

"I texted him after I got rid of my sling but he didn't reply."

"Oh no," says Imelda. "Maybe—"

"His dog died?" I say. "His phone broke?"

"Okay, that does sound stupid."

"Want a ride home?" asks Noor.

"Nah, I'm good." I wait for them to leave, then shower at the gym. All the other girls have gone home and I'm here alone.

Jason's waiting for me by the train station. "You're mad," he says, a bit shy.

"No."

"Yes, you are." He runs a hand through his hair, and I remember what it felt like under my fingers. Silky, for a guy. Silkier than mine, anyway. "School's been crazy. I'm sorry I never replied to the text you sent."

Yeah, well, I'm sorry I sent it. "Okay."

"Let me take you home," he says. "My car's just over there."

"You have a car?"

"My dad's car. I'm spending tonight at my parents' place, so he let me have it."

I want to be the kind of person that turns down a ride home on principle, but the truth is I'm really tired tonight and I don't want to take the train. Maybe the truth is about Jason, too. I don't know. We'll just have to see.

We get into his dad's car and he puts the seat warmer on for me. The stereo comes on automatically when he starts it, and pretty soon we're headed to my house, blasting reggaetón. College boy doesn't have bad taste in music, actually.

Instead of dropping me off in front of my house, he pulls into the parking lot, toward the far end where the forest begins. Switches off the car. Bye-bye reggaetón and hello awkward silence.

"So," Jason says.

If he thinks I'm going to bring up the subject of him checking out on me after sex, he's got another thing coming. I reach for the handle. "Thanks for the ride."

"Wait. Just gimme a sec here. I want to explain something. After that night you came over, I just felt . . . I don't know. Like it happened too fast, everything. Needed to figure some stuff out."

I have no idea what he's talking about. Aren't guys supposed to want it? And now he's here telling me that maybe he didn't? "If you have a girlfriend, you could have just told me."

He looks hurt. "I don't have a girlfriend. The last girl I dated . . . we broke up months ago, before I started coming to the gym. That's why I was into training so much. I was trying to get over her. Then I met you, but I hadn't really gotten over the breakup . . ."

Wow. "So I'm the rebound."

"I swear I never saw you that way, Trish. I was at the gym a lot. Kept seeing you train. There was something a little crazy about you."

"Did you just call me crazy?" All of a sudden I'm feeling mighty aggressive up in this car.

"Okay, sorry. Didn't mean it like that. I just meant fierce. I liked it. And I realized I liked you, too. I wasn't expecting to, but I did."

So much disappointment in just one conversation. I need a thousand hot showers to feel like myself again. Maybe I should ask Pammy if I can borrow her self-help books or something, get some enlightenment. He didn't expect to like me because why?

I kiss my teeth just like Ma would because that's the only response I can think of with as much disdain as I'm feeling. I'm about to get out of the car when he touches my shoulder lightly. "How's your arm feeling after all that training?"

"Don't worry about it. I can take care of myself."

He looks skeptical. "Yeah? Sometimes I see you whaling on the bag for so long, sparring all night, never holding anything back—it's like you're trying to hurt yourself. You're not doing this as a sport. It's not fun for you." He moves the hand to my shoulder, and it doesn't feel bad so I let him.

"It is fun for me," I say. "It's the only place where I have any control."

"Trish, you don't have control in a ring!"

That's true. I'm smiling now, and so is he. I can see that he feels bad about being kind of a jerk. "I'm really sorry about not being around as much. I do like you," he says.

"Why?"

"Why do I like you?"

I nod. I hope he doesn't call me crazy again.

"I don't know. Just do. Why do you like me?"

Is he high? "What makes you think—"

He kisses me then. And it feels just the same as the night in his dorm. Like I don't want him to stop. I suddenly understand that scene in that old *Titanic* movie Aunty K is shockingly still into, where the windows in the car heat up and the hand presses against the glass. Doing this in a car isn't as comfy as on the bed, but it definitely beats the train station and, all in all, is the nicest way I can think of for Jason to make it up to me.

We've been at it for a while when I see the headlights approaching. Another car pulls into the lot and parks in the space nearest to our unit. "Get down," I hiss at Jason, sliding lower in my seat and pulling him with me. "It's my mom."

"Are you not allowed to date or something?"

"No, I . . . It's complicated. My mom . . . she's just not ready to know."

We watch as Ma gets out of her car. She doesn't spare a glance our way, but the mood is killed.

"I gotta go," I say, pulling down my shirt. My hair is a tangled mess so I put it into a quick bun.

"Wait. That's it?"

And then I do get mad. So he's MIA for all this time and *now* he doesn't want me to leave? "Yeah, that's it. You bounced. I don't owe you anything."

"Okay, okay. I never said you did." He puts his hands up. He's gone quiet and serious now. "I know I messed up, but are we done here, me and you?"

Like I'm supposed to have all the answers all of a sudden. "I don't know. There's so much going on, especially now that I'm back training." As soon as I say it, I feel awful. But it's the truth.

He looks like I slapped him. "Right. Yeah. Of course. You have to train until you're falling over and practically dead. My bad."

"Are you jealous that I'm a better fighter than you?"

"Okay, I know you don't want me to call you crazy but honestly that's just ridiculous. I *like* that you can fight. That's not what this is about. Trish, I'm worried about you, okay?" He pulls me in for a hug, messing my hair up again. "It's like you got some kind of monster in you that you're trying to work out, but that would only make sense if it came out in the ring, which it doesn't. Maybe the little demos that don't matter, yeah, you win those, but the others? Where it's for real? It's like you switch off and let them hit you. It's like . . ." He pauses here, but he's come too far to stop now. "I don't know why Kru doesn't see it. Why he keeps letting you in the ring. Don't go to Florida, Trish."

"He believes in me!"

"He doesn't even see you."

But that's not true. He does. Kru knows I need this more than anything else.

Jason tries to say something else but I'm too angry to listen. I get out of the car this time.

Ma's door is closed so I shower and go to bed as quietly as I can. Jason calls but I turn off my phone before I'm tempted to answer. I'm still thinking about what he said. It's not possible that Kru doesn't see me. Because what else do I have but training and my ma, who's alone now even though Ravi is around. Ravi obviously doesn't count. And Ma . . . who does she have but a neighbor, a sister that lives in another country, and me?

And how else am I supposed to deal with the fact that I'm scared, all the time?

For her . . . and now . . .

Now I'm scared of her.

I go digging through Ravi's drawers in Ma's bedroom. She erased Dad from them ages ago and let Ravi keep little bits of himself in the places where Dad used to be. There's not much there. His work clothes. Heavy jeans and plaid shirts. Belts with makeshift notches in them to keep up with his shrinking waistline.

In the basement, I find his toolbox. I pull away tools sharp enough to break open a back door, a bed of nails, a bed of bolts. I'm about to give up when I see a leather pouch. What a weird place to hide photos, I think, until I look through them.

I'm alert to every sound in the townhouse unit. I feel not like myself, but someone sneakier, someone smarter. An investigative sort of person with nothing to lose, who's drunk off some kind of need to know.

I've never needed to know before, didn't want to know. But this new person I've become is a nosy bitch.

Crouching there like a wild animal, I scatter the photos in front of me and paw these images from the past. They're faded Polaroids from at least twenty years ago. Ravi as a teenager, at school. In front of a scooter. One at the beach with an arm slung around Ma's waist, her smiling up at him. The picture must be at least twenty years old because they're both young and beautiful here. I knew Ma must have always been fine—you can still see it now in her high cheekbones, in her big dark eyes and pouty lips. The figure barely contained by her pinstripe bikini. Ravi, though, I had no idea he used to look like this. Sort of cute. His brashness shines out at me.

I know dudes like this, have trained with them practically every day for years. They're the junk people, like me, who no one wants and have nowhere to go at the end of the day but the gym because it's the only place that will have them. This is the rough kind of guy who will spar you and hold nothing back until you're a puddle of sweat. They'll egg you on, cast doubt on your technique and try to own you when they hold pads for you but will unleash their full power when you're the one holding the pads. They'll try to break your wrists when you hold for them and laugh when a teep sends you flying. They'll sweep your legs from under you and pummel you at exercises that aren't even competitions.

When you're in the ring, though, when the stakes are high, they're the ones who'll have your back. But not without you putting in the hours with them first. Not without a price.

So Ravi had her back.

He was there with her in Trinidad, hearing the parrot squawk "Eliza is a whore" and he was in Diego Martin when my dad was attacked. He has her back and his price is that drawer upstairs and the groove in our sofa.

I put the photos back in the order I found them and close up the toolbox.

Ma, I think, *what's the price you make him pay?*

But I already know her price. She's making him disappear.

twenty-eight

Insert training montage. This is the part of the story where the underdog has something to prove to the world, the interlude before Rocky wins the big fight against Apollo Creed and shouts *Adrian!* into the crowd and slobbers all over her when she arrives at his side. This is what gets him to that point. When Samart Payakaroon's trainer tells him to work his jabs and teeps before his killer knockout sends Panomtoanlek Hapalang to the ground, choking on his own mouth guard.

This is the part where the coach says: *Alright, I'll train you, ya bum, but you gotta give me one hundred and ten percent. You hear? You hold nothing back and we'll see what you're made of.*

(You hope you're made of steel under your skin.)

Skip till you're cross-eyed, flicking the rope like a whip, crossing it, send it flying in time with your feet.

Work drills and drills and drills.

Spar with the best in the gym, who give you their everything because they can smell the hunger on you and they want to give it to you because everybody knows that there's nothing else but this.

Where you give Kru *your* everything because even though he's got woman troubles, you're not gonna be part of them.

This is the part where you lose yourself to that hunger and even though they say you gotta give them the whole of what you got, your one-ten, it's really about taking. You're taking everything they have so they, all of them in your ratty little eastside gym with the duct tape peeling off every hastily repaired surface, can live for a moment in your glory.

When you come alive in the ring and hear the crowd chant your name.

When you hold that gaudy-ass belt up over your head and know this moment is yours and no one can ever take it away from you.

Florida is in a couple days and people are definitely noticing the bruises. The ones on my arms and legs are a sinister rainbow of red, purple, yellow, green. Every color you can imagine is represented somewhere on my body. But I'm looking at the ones on my neck in the gym mirror out on the training floor. Junior's mom said a soucouyant was biting me, and I can see now why she'd think that, what with the marks on my throat, all angry and red.

Then I turn away, back to the giant tire in the middle of the floor, squat in front of it and lift it, exploding up on my haunches, my shoulders working in sync with my hips to throw it forward. It slams into the mat in front of me and I grin at the sound, moving with it to start all over again.

Jason's not around. So it's Ricky who holds mitts for me in the ring to work my precision. We're grunting through combos until we're both lathered in sweat and the humidity is rising up from the gym floor to meet the drops of perspiration falling from our brows. "Killer," he says. "Killer instinct."

"I think you're ready, Lucky," says Kru, who looks over from the floor. I may be banged up, but I look tight and everyone at the gym knows it. I smile so wide you can see all my teeth, which I still have. (Unlike some of the others.) It seems like everyone on the street knows it, too. A group of girls at the train station eye-fuck me and I can tell they're thinking of starting something. Usually I turn away from girls like that, they're not worth the trouble, but today I stand and stare at them, daring them closer. The train comes and takes them away, but I saw the look in their eyes, I saw the leader, the big one with the thin hair, think twice.

Ma looks at these bruises on my neck but says nothing. She can't see the ones on the rest of my body because I've taken to wearing sweats inside the house, no matter what the thermostat is set to.

"How is school?" she asks.

"Good." The teachers have given up on the graduating class. They know we're not listening to them anymore. If we don't have it by now, we'll never get it in these last six weeks before school ends. Homework is a joke, but I still pretend to do it every day to make Ma happy. "I got accepted into Ryerson. The letter came in the mail last week."

She lights up, grabs me by the shoulders, then remembers my acromioclavicular separation when I wince. "I'm so sorry, baby." She clutches me to her. "I'm happy for you, though! Ryerson! That's where you want to go, right?"

I nod and pull her fingers away from me. I don't want her to touch me. It feels so different from when she used to rub coconut oil through my hair. It's like something about me has changed, or maybe something about her has. Her nails are too sharp now. I can feel them even through my sweatshirt. But we're still close and I see her eyes on my skin, just below my ear.

She says nothing about the marks on me but I know she's worried because she cooks day and night, it seems. She cooks like a woman possessed by the spices in her cupboard. You want this? You want that? I'll make it right now, straight away.

She gives me iron tablets one day. "Your iron is low."

What is she talking about? How could she know?

After that she tries to get me to eat this gross blood pudding. I gag on it. It tastes fresh and nasty in my mouth. I watch as she eats the portion on her plate, spreads it on a cracker and shoves the whole thing in her mouth. Even Ravi seems disgusted, but he's even weaker than I am so he can't say anything.

My lunchtime Desis are horrified by me in a T-shirt, I can tell. "Earth to Trisha," says Parminder, the loudest one in the group. That's not saying much, as they're all pretty loud when they want to be. But Parminder is by far the loudest. I look up from my cards. "How's your arm?" she asks.

Unconsciously, I rotate my shoulders. The muscles of my biceps press against my shirt. The girls stare at the veins in my arms, the type you usually only see on very hot guitar players. "Good."

We go back to our cards, but I can feel them sneaking glances. Sharp eyes in their soft faces. Soft bodies, too, moving like sludge through the hallways. They pick up other topics. Everyone got into the university of their choice, except for Rina, who chose to take a year to work and go to beauty school instead. Her dream is to wax the hair off of ladies while they scream (I assume) and we all pretend we don't pity her, but we do. Even me, covered in bruises.

I run into Mr. Abdi in the hall outside the English department. There's something haunted in his eyes when he looks at me. "You alright, Trisha?"

"All good, Mr. Abdi." This is the second time I've said this today, that I'm alright. "I was wondering . . . the soucouyant book . . . can I borrow it? I can give it back next week."

He goes into the office and comes back out with the slim novel. "Here, you can keep it. I insist. I love that book, you know. Maybe it will spark something for you the second read—if you make it all the way through. It's about time we get some more diverse literature into the hands of students, teach them about other kinds of stories. Show them they have a place in the world of storytelling, too." He rambles on for a bit about this diversity stuff and says things like "representation" and "inclusion."

Yeah, okay.

I clutch the book to my chest. He can't stop looking at my neck. I pull up the hood of my sweatshirt and bunch it around my shoulders. "I'm training a lot," I explain.

"Maybe you should make another appointment with the guidance counselor. It might be good to talk to someone about . . . your training."

He sounds like Jason.

I go to the gym and there's just something about my focus that's not showing up anywhere else. If I'm weak, it's everywhere but here. Which is strange, because everything at the gym reminds me of Jason. Speaking of. He's been trying to reach me but I still don't know what to say. I ignore all his calls, his texts. Sometimes I want to talk to him so bad, to just chill in his dorm for a bit, but it's impossible after what he said about my training.

I'm thinking maybe he quit the gym for a while, but then

there's the fighter's demo for the upcoming season. I'm wrapping my hands for a little sparring session and feel like someone's watching me.

Jason.

He looks tired, but alright. He nods to me once, then turns to say something to Kru. Then they both look at me. I continue wrapping and step into the ring with Amanda like there's no one else in the world but me and her.

Kru keeps staring, though. As if he's considering me. Doubting me.

I find Jason after, in the men's change room. "What did you say to him?" I push him. Not hard, but hard enough. We're alone, so it's fine.

But apparently it's not fine to him. "Don't touch me if you're gonna do shit like that," he says. He goes to the door. "I told him the truth. Something's up with you. I don't think you should be fighting."

"Stay out of it!" I push him again. He doesn't like it, but we aren't in the ring and he won't do anything about it when we aren't geared up.

"I will from now on. You need help. You hit your head one too many times or something."

What, so I'm brain-dead now? I've got CTE like those football players? Chronic traumatic ence-something (I can't remember exactly—but that DOES NOT mean I actually do have CTE).

"Wait," I say.

He turns. "What?" He looks really angry, for some reason. I don't know why. If anyone has a reason to be mad, it's me. Talking to Kru behind my back like a snitch? That's just straight-up wrong. If he really cared about me, he wouldn't have said anything.

He waits for a moment, but I guess I don't have anything to say to him, really, so he just leaves.

I wish I could talk to him without fighting.

A minute later Ricky comes in, sees me on the bench. I'm wide open, legs apart, like I've just been hit. "I would," he says, smirking, "but you're not my type."

For the life of me I can't think of a comeback. I try real hard, but my mind can't seem to hold on to anything right now.

"Kru wants to see you," says Ricky. I wait till he leaves, then I knock on Kru's door and stick my head inside. I see him put a photo back into his desk drawer. He shuts the drawer and clears his throat. There's a spreadsheet open on his computer screen and a selection of vitamin water on the shelf behind him.

My mouth is dry, but my palms are sweating. I'm still wearing my hand wraps, but I wish I'd taken them off. From the way that Kru is not looking at me, I already know what he's going to say.

"Trisha . . ."

He never calls me this. Well, not never. The last time was when he found out my dad died and he said *Trisha, I'm sorry.* But I can't remember any time before that, it's been so long.

"Look, I'm just going to tell it plain. You're off the card for Florida. Trisha, I'm sorry." There it is again.

I stagger into the room. "Kru, please don't."

He shakes his head. "It's not the right time. I already pulled you."

"Well, put me back!"

"No."

"Is it because of Jason? Because, Kru, I think he's mad at me because I broke up with him. He doesn't know anything!"

He blinks. I don't think he even knew there was a thing between me and Jason, though it was obvious to just about everyone else.

This scorned woman line doesn't work on him. "You can still come with us to Miami but no fighting."

"Kru, I swear I can do this."

"I know you can. I wouldn't have put you on the card if I didn't think so. But I'm not going to let you this time. We'll get you ready for the next tournament. You can come with us to support. The team would like you there." He says this last part quietly. He never speaks to me this way. With caution.

I can't be in here anymore, so I leave. Outside, in the back lot, I put my fist into the brick wall. Blood wells at my knuckles and there's a sharp stab in my wrist but the pain is nothing new. I feel it and I know I'll feel it more in a minute, but for right now I barely let in anything but the rage. I don't even feel the cold, which still lingers even though it's supposed to be spring.

There's a sound behind me like the clearing of a throat. Imelda's standing there, looking at me. I didn't even hear her approach. "What?"

"Kru told me that I'm replacing you in Florida. I just want to make sure you're okay."

Imelda is replacing me? What a surprise.

"Yeah, I look it, don't I?" I bite out.

She doesn't flinch, just stares at me with those big blue eyes that seem to follow me wherever I go. I try to push her from my mind, even though she's right in front of me. I can't help picture her with Kru in Florida. Without me. Imelda, Amanda and Noor competing for a belt.

"You should take care of that hand," she says. "I hope you still come with us for the trip, Lucky."

"Don't call me that."

"Whatever." She frowns, not liking what she hears in my voice, but I've just about had it with people messing with me. I don't care if she likes it or not.

"You're a crazy fucking bitch, aren't you?" she says suddenly. It's the most un-Imelda-like thing I've ever heard anyone say, least of all Imelda herself. Outside of the gym walls, it seems like we've become different people, the two of us. And maybe everyone else goes through this meta-morphosis, too. Slip off one face and put on another. What do any of us know about each other, other than what we learn in training? I used to think it was our real selves that came through on the mat, in the ring. Hide away all the masks under a layer of hand wraps, keeping them bound until you leave again.

But now I feel like an idiot because Imelda standing there and calling me a crazy fucking bitch like it's nothing says that everything we are in the gym together is just a big fat lie. She had no trouble taking my spot in the tourna-ment, either. I imagine that Noor and Amanda would be better. That they'd turn it down, but I know they wouldn't. A chance to win a belt? Make Kru proud? Nobody's saying no to that.

"Go eat something, Lucky. You're too skinny." She walks away and it's a good thing, too, because I want nothing more than to show her what this skinny fucking crazy bitch still has left.

Fuck her, I think, as I watch her go, her red hair streaming behind her. Fuck her and Kru, too. That nickname has never seemed more like a joke. Lucky, huh? When have I *ever* been that? Ma says I was born at three forty-eight on a Monday morning. The witching hour, and that could explain it all. I'm nothing but black magic, dark portents, bad juju. Take your chances on anyone but me.

My hand stings but at least there are no broken bones. Maybe just a sprain if I'm lucky, which, clearly I've never been. I don't want to put my fist into another wall. No way. I want the feel of skin tearing. I want to see fear. I want to see my rage reflected back at me.

That's what I want.

My phone rings. It's Jason.

twenty-nine

Jason comes down to let me into his dorm, and I'm still thrumming with anger. The spring chill froze it in place inside my body, but as I follow him up the stairs I feel it thaw and run warm again. We take the back stairs, but don't pass anyone on the way up. He tells me earlier the term is ending and most of the other students in his dorm have already started moving out. But he's got late exams, so he's still here for another few days.

I'm tired. My anger has now run right through me and disappeared. Just one look at his sleepy face and red-rimmed eyes and I know I don't want anything to do with his pain, even with all he's taken away from me.

When he sees my hand with cuts on my knuckles already scabbing over, he blinks back shock and rummages through his drawer until he comes out with a box of tiny bandages. None of them are big enough to cover the cuts, but he layers a few over my hand anyway. He puts the box away. We don't say anything for a long time. I don't want to tear his skin off and I don't know what the hell I'm doing here, I just feel . . . I just feel.

Imelda was right. I *am* a crazy fucking bitch.

Finally: "He took me off the card for Florida. You did that."

He has the decency to look ashamed. "I was worried about you. He asked me how I thought you were looking out there at the demo and I couldn't lie."

Everyone's so worried all of a sudden that I wonder where it's all coming from. Ever since Dad died the world's turned upside down.

Jason takes my hand. "Does it hurt?"

I shake my head. "Not much."

"So tough," he grins. "Here." He hands me a Tylenol. I wash it down with some water. "You should go home and get some sleep."

"I don't want to go home."

He doesn't look at me for a while. Like Kru in the office.

I just sit there like a loser until he pulls back the covers on his tiny bed and gets in, leaving a space for me. When I get in, his arms come around me and he presses a kiss to my temple, where that girl hit me once. The exact spot my head-gear had slipped and lost me the fight, her fist plowing straight into the soft tissue there.

"You're burning up," he says, reaching over to open a window.

Am I? I don't feel hot at all.

A breeze comes through. The room is so tiny that it takes

no time at all to cool it down. For just that moment it feels like we're the only two people in the world. Everything feels sort of smudgy, like we're in a painting or something. Not in the real world. I slide a hand under his T-shirt so I can feel the muscles in his back. It still feels nice.

We fall asleep just like that.

I'm dreaming. Floating in a sea of red. I feel something bite me and, with a slap, pull my hand away to find a dead mosquito. The slap wakes me, but it takes a full minute to figure out where I am. I hear someone breathing nearby and I am seized with this feeling. Like I've got to be quiet, or else. Shhh, if you stay still like that no one will notice you. He won't hit you if he doesn't know you're here. If he doesn't know you're here, he'll only see her. I shut my eyes tight, but I still see the red.

I hear a voice. "What's wrong?"

I don't open my eyes or move.

"Hey, Trish?" I feel someone stir beside me. In the bed, beside me. Then Jason's hand rests on my arm and I relax. "Want me to call your mom? You're so hot. I think you have a fever."

"No, don't call her!" I say. I can't help the fear in my voice. I know he's heard it, too.

He pauses. All his attention focuses on me in the dark. "Is there something wrong? Trish?" When there's no response, he brushes a lock of hair from my face. "How did you hurt your arm?"

"Fell down the stairs."

He knows I'm lying. I don't know how. Maybe I was talking in my sleep. Maybe in my sleep I let all my secrets hang out to dry before shoving them back in again in the morning. Guys shouldn't know how to read girl-secrets but Jason somehow does and it isn't fair, because he doesn't stop with just the one.

"How did your dad die?"

I say nothing.

"Trish? Hey, talk to me."

You'd think that fear would make me keep my mouth shut, but it has the opposite effect. It makes me want to tell him everything. "I killed him," I whisper. "I was driving and it was raining and I didn't mean to, he just appeared out of nowhere, like he came at us—"

"I don't believe you! I don't believe a word you say. Why are you lying?"

Shut up shut up shut up shut up shut up shut up shut up . . .

"She told me to."

Damn it.

There's a coldness now as he takes his heat away from my side. He switches on his desk lamp. "I'm going to call the cops."

"And tell them what?"

"You can't . . . you don't deserve this. You're so stressed out, Trish. I'm going to call *someone*."

"No!" I get up. I see him there, looking so angry and confused, and I want his heat back, pressed into me, and I remember what it was like the night we had sex. Like I could stay here forever. I want it again, that feeling. So I kiss him, but he pushes me off.

For the first time ever, it's like he's stronger than me.

"I don't want to take advantage of you," he says, but all I hear is *I don't want*.

"It doesn't feel right?" I sling his own words back at him and watch as I hit my target, center of the mitt.

He flinches. "Trish . . . your dad just died. You're going through something and I don't understand it at all."

I turn away. Suddenly, I can't stand the sight of him. I feel stupid, so stupid, as I wrench the door open and rush down the stairs of his dorm.

Now there's no anger keeping me warm, only shame and this feeling like I betrayed her. I can't stand the thought. Who'll take care of her if Jason calls the cops and they split us apart? I don't even know who *they* are, but the thought of her alone is enough to make me feel sick to my stomach.

Ma comes in from work just after I reach home. I don't know where Ravi is.

"Went to the bank today." She takes out a few bills from her purse and puts them on the kitchen table for me. My arm is better, but it's like she still sees me falling down the stairs every time she looks at me. I take the money, though. Slip it into my pocket and she nods, almost like she's grateful. "You hungry?"

"Yeah," I say. I am. I realize I'm starving.

She fries up some bake and cuts a block of cheddar into thin slices to go with it. As I watch her clatter about the kitchen, her movements slow but precise, my appetite vanishes—

This is the last thing I made for him. Dad.

—and I can't swallow because he's still here, hasn't gone away, is in everything she does even with Ravi around. I look up from the bake to see her watching me, a strange sort of knowing look in her eyes. The money burns my pocket, sears through the lining to get at my bruised skin.

"Do you remember your dreams?" I ask her, desperate for an answer, any answer.

She looks at me for a long time, under the dent in the wall, now immortalized by the rolling pin she hurled at my head, just looks and looks and doesn't end up finding what she's searching so hard for. "You're too weak for this country, girl."

Weak? Excuse her. Has she seen me train?

She watches me eat every bite of the bake she put on my plate and is only satisfied when I press the crumbs to my lips and thank her. I hate the meekness in my voice, but it's what she wants to hear. How dutiful I am, how grateful. How glad for all the sacrifices she makes for me, even the ones I don't ask for.

That releases her to bed.

When she's gone, I go to the cupboard and fill my pocket with salt. Later, in the bathroom, I put some of the salt in a glass of water and retch up everything I ate. Feel my strength return with every bite of food I bring back up. Like it's poison, the food made by her hand turning to bile in my throat.

I see my face in the mirror and, maybe it's because a bulb or two have blown in here, but whatever it is, I have lost most of my color. I look bloodless, pale, like my stores of melanin somehow deserted me. I look like her a little bit even. This is the face I wanted to tear off. Not Jason's.

I'm sad about Jason. I text him to tell him I'm sorry leaving the way I did. He doesn't respond after an hour, so I tell myself that he's not my type. I mean, I don't exactly know what my type is, but it's definitely not a guy who doesn't text back.

Back in my room, I close the curtains. With my stomach empty I feel free, light. If the Brazilian girl was in the ring with me now, she wouldn't stand a chance. I'd be so fast now. I put away the money, adding it to the stack of bills already in there. It's more than I ever earned in my two years at Foot Locker, that's for sure.

For a moment, I stand in front of my closet. Just looking. The pink graduation dress hangs toward the back, looking more and more like a cake every day that goes by. When I slide my wiry body into it, it's a sad cake that sags in the middle, like the baker dolloped extra icing on to hide how bad it is.

I take a pair of scissors to it.

In minutes, it becomes a pile of ragged pink strips shoved under my bed.

Now I can turn back to the money I stashed. I put it all in my bag, every cent. It's enough, I think. I already have the plane ticket in my name. This could get me through Florida. The insurance papers I photocopied from the ones Ma has in the bank are hidden in the deep sleeve pocket in my backpack. There's my dad's name again, right on those papers. I stare at it for a long time, then I put the papers back into the envelope.

That night, I spill the salt from my pocket along the edge of the door to keep the dreams away. Look, I know it's dumb but I do it anyway. It makes me feel better.

"Ravi," I whisper, crouching beside the couch before I leave. His eyes are closed. I don't know if he can hear me, but I've got to try. I don't dare touch him, though. "Ravi, go away."

He doesn't stir.

"She doesn't want you here. She won't stand for it any more. Ravi, go home."

His eyelids flutter. I don't touch him. "Go home, Ravi."

Still nothing. I look at the clock. I have to go.

I tuck the envelope with Dad's life insurance papers into his shirt, sling my backpack over my shoulder and leave without locking the door behind me. I want him to see what she's done. I want him to know she doesn't really want him.

thirty

Kru is unhappy I came with them to Florida. I guess he didn't actually think I would. Imelda's pissed. Amanda and Noor hugged me at the airport when they saw me, and we weren't even clinching.

I wait until the team has registered and weighed in, then slip downstairs to the registration desk. I give the man behind the desk my name. He says I'm not on the list. I say of course I am and show him the confirmation email on my phone from Kru, before he kicked me off the team. The man checks his list again, doesn't see me. He calls a woman over. She's got a lanyard with the tournament logo on it and, just below, the name *Rashida*.

Rashida is the floor manager. She has dreads down to her waist, bruised elbows and a cut on her chin that can only mean one thing. She's a fighter, too. I could tell her a sad story about how my father died and my mother has turned into an evil monster and I broke my arm and this guy I liked wouldn't even have sex with me to make up for it and that I've been training for this for ages and Imelda shows up one day and suddenly I'm on the outs . . . but she won't care about any of that.

She looks through her emails and finds a thread about me. "You were on the card, but your coach pulled you."

"No, he didn't."

"Says right here he did."

I shake my head. "Nobody told me anything."

"Well, that's too bad because you're not on the card anymore. We don't have space for you."

"I came here to fight. I want a fight."

"Honey, this is not a game you want to play with me." She stares at me, but I don't flinch. The guy who called her over clears his throat, but neither of us pay him any attention.

"All my paperwork was sent in. I'm ready."

"I can see that," she says slowly. Then she points to a couch just off the lobby. "Go sit over there."

"I want—"

"Yeah, I heard. What I want is for you to sit your narrow ass on that couch until I check on one of the other fighters who didn't make weight. She's gonna try again in an hour, and if she still doesn't make it, you're in. So don't test me right now. I might be the best friend you ever had."

On the couch, I slink down into the cushions, pulling my hood up. My phone buzzes but I don't answer. Kru, Amanda, Noor and Imelda walk right past without recognizing me. An hour passes, then another one. I'm hungry, but there's no chance that I'm eating now. I fall asleep and when I wake up Rashida is standing over me, frowning. "Ready, huh?"

"I am," I say, clearing my throat and sitting up.

"Good. Go weigh in then. And, after that, eat a couple sandwiches, would ya?"

I can't keep the stupid grin off my face as I promise that I'll eat as many sandwiches as she wants.

I make weight, then eat three tuna sandwiches.

The next day, my phone keeps ringing but I switch it off. I'm fighting a Sri Lankan girl from Iowa first up. I didn't know there were Sri Lankans in Iowa, but now's not the time to think about details like that. I see her shadowboxing in the locker room area. She's shorter than me, but wider. Her neck and shoulders are powerful, but her legs are like sticks.

I warm up with Noor and Amanda. They think it's about solidarity. Kru's holding mitts for Imelda, who pretty much ignores me. Maybe she's hoping my crazy won't rub off on her. They all get a sense of just what a crazy fucking bitch I am when Rashida comes in and calls my name, along with the Sri Lankan girl's. Tells us we're up next.

Kru is so shocked he just trails behind me. Then I'm in the ring, doing my Wai Kru to pay my respects. While I do that, he seems to get a grip on himself and hops up into my corner. Something in his eyes promises we're gonna have a talk about this later, but there is no later when you're about to fight a Sri Lankan with toothpicks for legs and thick, muscular arms.

"Don't let her land any punches," he says, before the bell goes.

She comes at me from the jump. This is Noor's style, too, so it's like I've already sparred this girl a million times. I move my head just a fraction and feel her right cross go plowing past me, all power. She's off balance, so I step to the left and get a swing kick in, right to her skinny thigh. Her knee buckles and she almost drops. I follow with a push kick to her belly and she falls on her ass, looking up at me, stunned.

And never gets over that humiliation. She tries, but this is a lesson I've learned over and over, that when your confidence gets shook in the ring, there's no coming back. The crowd flips on you in that moment.

There's no loyalty in a crowd.

Loyalty doesn't even have a place here. No matter if they were on your side at the beginning, they turn on you quick as lightning. They want strength. They want to see power. So I dominate her for the rest of the fight. She lands one solid punch, a hook to my jaw, and though my head spins, I have the sense at least to pull her in for a knee and push her back to take another swing to her thigh, working the same spot I first hit. Making the bruise bigger, redder, angrier. I work it till it turns purple and she's out of breath from carrying her thick arms on those thin little legs and she's almost grateful when the final bell calls it. Her arms are so heavy with defeat that when the ref throws my hand up at the end of the match, hers hang so low they might as well be planted in the floor covering.

Kru wants to have it out with me, but Imelda's up next and he doesn't have the time. Ma keeps calling, but I can't answer. I feel her anger pulsing out at me. Junior calls, but I don't know what to say to him, either.

Nothing from Jason.

Columbus is the only one I can bear talking to. "Where are you?" he asks, as soon as I answer. "Your mom is going crazy over here. You disappeared and she can't find Ravi, either."

"I'm at a tournament. What do you mean she can't find Ravi?"

"He hasn't been at your house since yesterday. You need to come back, Trish. Your mom—"

I don't want to hear about her so I hang up. Head downstairs with vague thoughts of finding something to eat. A wave of heat licks me from head to toe as soon as I step outside, so I retreat and eat at the hotel restaurant. Miami is in between hurricanes at the moment, so the sun is shining extra bright. It's unbearable, this light in my eyes. Switching tables to the darkest corner of the restaurant helps a little.

The team joins me. Kru sits across from me and watches me eat my burger. I don't flinch. He sighs heavily. I think he's starting to regret training girls in the first place, but we've all won our first matches so he's battling with his pride, too.

Pride wins out.

He doesn't curse me out, just says, "Don't ever do that again." And everything's okay between us.

The other fighters seem relieved. With our hair in braids, our hard thighs in satin shorts the brightest colors of the rainbow, the firm set of our mouths and the wildness in our eyes, we are all crazy fucking bitches here.

Imelda warms me up before my next fight. We're good. I think she's trying hard to make it like it used to be but I don't care about all that because I'm about to get in the ring again and there's no space inside me for anything but the rush. At the end of this fight there'll hopefully be another, and at the end of that one a big black-and-gold belt. Noor got knocked out of the tourney an hour ago. Right now I'd rather die than be her.

We were all out there cheering for her, but it wasn't enough. She faced the Brazilian chick from Buffalo who's fighting here too, and who I guess has it out for our gym because she demolished Noor in a series of clinches that sapped the strength from her body like it was wisps of cotton candy. Nobody could be bothered to feel too sorry for Noor, either, because we're already looking ahead. Well, me at least. Imelda, I guess, is trying to be a generally better person (what a time for it, Jesus) and keeps sending Noor consoling smiles, even as she holds mitts for me.

I push it all aside.

My second fight is against a towering brunette who's all leg and hair. Thin, ropey muscles on her legs and stomach and not a pinch of fat anywhere else. Hard look in her eyes. It should have been outlawed for her to fight based on weight rather than height. At least that's what I think before the second round starts. The first round was solid and we both landed a few good points, but you could tell that she isn't used to fighting someone who isn't intimidated by her size. She tried to get me into a clinch a few times, but I'd just seen Noor fall for that and I didn't let her anywhere close. I was ready for it, ready for this to be the longest fight of my life, to keep light, keep scoring.

"Points," Kru whispered to me, taking my head between his hands after the first-round bell. "Play this one smart, Lucky. Think about your injury, okay? Protect yourself."

But there isn't time for that, because Amazon rushes me at the third bell and I take a straight elbow to my nose. Blood gushes all over my face, my gloves when I bring my hands up, the mat when it drips down my chin. My eyes go soft, blurry. I grab the rope with one gloved hand but slip and go down to my knee. I see her over me and I think, yes. Do it. She sees the defeat in my eyes, that I'm ready for it, blood sticky on my face and my nose in the wrong place. Then she's not there anymore. It's the ref, pulling her away, calling the match.

I feel Kru in the ring beside me before I see him, shouting about the illegal elbow. The other coach pulls Amazon down from her corner and shuffles her away from the ring.

I win by disqualification. It doesn't feel good, but I'll take it.

Imelda takes one look at my bloody face, goes pale and spontaneously develops cramps so severe that she goes upstairs, curls into the bathtub with a hot water bottle and won't come out again no matter how hard Noor bangs on the door.

When she does finally come out, there's color in her face again and she looks relaxed. I'm missing half of the painkillers that I'd left in the bathroom, the ones I stole from Ma's hoard of extra-strengths, and I guess I know what happened to them. Relaxed Imelda is better than her other versions, but I wish she hadn't popped so many of my pills. I could use some extra relaxation right about now.

Kru's guiding me to the doctor downstairs, but I can't chance they'll take me out of the tourney because of a broken nose so I leave him and am pushing my nose back into place with my hands. And if that pain isn't enough, I'm spotting, even though I haven't had a period in months. It happens sometimes while training, a blow will shake some extra blood loose down there and you just accept it and try to block better. But all this blood seems like a bad sign. I try to ignore it while I go down to the restaurant for dinner.

Iron, I think, and always protein. So I order a steak, medium-rare, because I heard the man next to me order the same thing. When it comes, I'm not disgusted by the red meat like I usually am. Imelda takes one look at me chewing that juicy slab, cutting it into little pieces and scooping mashed potatoes onto the fork between bites, and she all but throws up. One second she's there and then she's not and it's just me and Amanda. Kru has taken Noor for a walk to cheer her up. I don't miss them. Sometimes it's good to disappear.

When Kru comes back, he takes me aside and urges me not to fight in the final. Something about it not being the right time with my broken nose and I'm looking weak. Some other stuff in there, too. I watch his mouth move and think about how wrong Jason was. Kru does care. It's so sweet. I nod and tell him I'll think about it.

I sleep for ten hours straight. I'm sharing a bed with Amanda, but I don't even feel her next to me. I sleep like the dead. Not the cursed or the haunted. I fall into a place where dreams can't find me. I'm too far away for a ball of fire to shoot across the sky. It's searching, even I know that, but the distance is too much for that obeah magic to reach. I'm safe. I may look weak, but I've never felt stronger. Good thing, too, because I'm going to fight the Brazilian chick from Buffalo in the morning. I can't lose to her again. It'll be the last fight of the tournament, and I can't wait for my chance at that belt.

There's nothing else.

thirty-one

The ring girl slides between the ropes, all silky-like. Her tits are high and hard-looking, but I'm guessing people dig that because they cheer like she's just launched a rocket into space or something when all she's done is hold up a card and twitch her butt. She's fit enough to maybe be a fighter, with a solid pair of calves, so what's she doing with this crap? Her self-respect must have fallen somewhere under the waistband of her thong. I hope she can dig it out again.

She makes a round with the card held over her head, in high heels on a mat that I'll walk barefoot. Gross. It's the last fight of the tournament, *the* fight of the tournament, and it seems like everyone is out here watching. Everyone but Amanda, who lost her fight earlier to a Thai girl from New Jersey. Last I saw her she went for a walk and hasn't come back. No matter. I've got Imelda and Noor, who are in my corner with Kru.

I turn my back to the ring while Kru adjusts my headgear. Run my tongue around my mouth guard, feeling its familiar bumps and ridges curling under my lips, creating bulges that my mouth can't quite close over. It's easy to growl with your mouth guard in; you're already halfway there.

The lights over the ring are so bright, like they turned them up just for this moment, to make me squint as I see the pink satin panels of the Brazilian fighter's Thai skirt whirl as she turns, revealing muscular legs dotted with purpling bruises. Her skirt distracts from them, whereas my plain black shorts with gold piping do nothing to hide the abuse. We're matched in height and weight, but the veins in her arms are like angry blue rivers, prominent and bursting.

I've replayed the video of our last fight so much that I feel like I know her. I've seen some of her other fights, too, and just watched her demolish Noor. She exists in my head, a quick-footed hologram with devastating blows that should be too powerful for her frame. And now she's put on about five pounds of muscle while I've lost about the same. When we touch gloves, she says "back for more?" and slips my jab that comes whipping at her face. She returns for a cross, but I'm ready for her speed and dodge that one.

She grabs my next swing kick and pushes me into the ropes with my right leg tucked up into her armpit. I feel her going to sweep my left leg under me, so I bend the right and launch the left up on the other side of her waist, which sends her backward under the weight of my body and lets me get my arms around her in a clinch. My feet find the floor. I don't get the plum, though, her crown just out of reach as she pushes me off. I made her mad with the move off the ropes so she comes at me full power for the rest of the round. I'm so tired from the chase that I need the rest before the bell goes again. Kru's hands on my shoulders, loosening them. "Points, Lucky. No more fancy stuff."

He doesn't have to worry. The second round is more chase. She gets a hook in to my temple, to the place I got hit once before, where I went plummeting to the mat and felt my head was going to explode. It's much worse this time, and I'm almost counted out. I wake when the ref shouts "seven" and stagger to my feet by "nine."

Something isn't right. I see little flashes of pink swirling. But I can't focus. I move away from the pink, just managing to stay out of reach for the rest of the round.

The bell goes and I'm back with Kru. He takes my head between his hands and looks me in the eye. "Do you want me to stop this?"

I blink away the sweat from my eyes. Over his shoulder, I see an old woman who looks like someone I used to know. It takes me a moment to realize it could be Ma, maybe is Ma, staring at me with hot lasers for eyes, burning through me. My knees buckle and Kru puts his hands under my shoulders to shore me up. I see him trying to get the ref's attention but the bell rings. Before he can stop me, I step away from him, turn my back on the woman—

I'm dead I'm dead I'm dead I'm dead I'm dead I'm dead I'm dead I'm dead I'm dead I'm dead

—and make sure my guard is up by the time Pink Skirt comes flying at me with a push kick. I turn to the side with a quick flick of my hip and land a swing kick to the back of her knees. She falls to the mat but is back up in a fraction of a second. The fall shook her, though, because she pulls back, turns mean. I block a punching combo and her movements have us turned away from the ref when she lands an illegal elbow to my broken nose.

The ref doesn't see. I hear Kru shouting behind me and the crowd up in arms, but some of them like it because now there's blood all down my face and, some of them, that's what they came for—

I'm dead I'm dead I'm dead I'm dead I'm dead I'm dead I'm dead I'm dead I'm dead

No, but I could be.

—I can feel her setting up for the hook, her secret weapon that's not-so-secret to me because I've watched her land it over and over on screen, the force of her blow spinning me one-eighty before I crash to the ground. So I slip it and put everything I have into an uppercut into her ribs. She steps back. I follow and pull her into a clinch and this time I do get her head between my gloves, enough to pull her face down into my knee.

The bell goes.

She springs away from me. I stand there bloody and confused, my nose flattened to my face. Feel the eyes, always on me and remember, suddenly, Ma's face in the crowd. I look, but don't see her. Sway toward the ropes, toward Kru who catches me just as my legs give out.

The judges are arguing over the illegal elbow, my second of the tournament. One of them saw it, but the others and the ref didn't. There's a bit of shouting happening between them—I think one of them is drunk. Somebody screams, "Storm's coming. Get on with it!" and finally they decide on a tie.

Noor squirts some water into my mouth from a squeeze-top bottle and Kru pushes me toward the center of the ring. Pink Skirt and I grip opposite ends of a big black belt. Neither of us smile, but we hold it up. The crowd claps and there are some cheers. Some jeers, too. I search the faces. Blink to clear my vision. The lights, they're so bright. So hot. Beads of sweat at my temple, and I'm shaking under the weight of the belt. Pink Skirt drops her end and disappears through the ropes.

The ring girl with decent calves appears from nowhere, wraps an arm around my waist and kisses my cheek for the crowd. She's holding me up, some kind of angel. I feel ashamed that I had nasty thoughts about her when the match started. "It's okay, hon, we'll get you to the doctor," she says. "Come on. I'll help you."

She helps me down from the ring. I see Rashida the floor manager beckoning me, the doctor right beside her. I turn away from them, away from the chaos of the match. I can't see her, Ma, but I can feel her, and that's even worse.

thirty-two

Upstairs in the room, I shower quickly and throw everything into my bags. There's a knock on the door. I pad toward it, bare feet making no sound at all on the carpeted floors. I press my palms against the door and listen. Someone is breathing on the other side. A harsh, ragged breath, uneven.

This is what I'm thinking: nobody with good intentions breathes like that at a hotel door.

Myself, I breathe through my mouth because my nose is too smashed to suck any air in and I think that a fragment of bone must have slid up into my brain because I call out "Who's there?" in a voice that's too tiny to be my own. I don't want to know who's there; I mean, I already know it. This whole thing starts to feel like something out of a horror film. I try to force myself to look through the peephole in the door, but the fear is too much for me and whatever bit of courage I had a moment ago—

Calling out *who's there* like an idiot

—disappears. If I put my eye to that little round window, glass will fly out at me, I know it. It will lodge in my brain, along with the shard of bone from my broken nose. I shut

my eyes tight and slip into the corner behind the door, waiting with my hands clenched into proper fists.

I wait.

She waits.

The breathing stops or she moves away. I hear someone
else coming down the hallway toward my door. Two sets
of footsteps, actually, and now I'm thinking this is like a real
movie, where the villain gets chased away by some bumbling passerby or something. Except it's not some bumbling
passerby at all. It's the people I thought had my back.

Amanda: " . . . I don't know."

Imelda: "She keeps hitting her head. She's not right. I saw
her punch a wall. She almost fucked up her hand."

Amanda: "*Something's* not right."

(Sound of some rifling. Things being pulled out of bags.
Some choice curse words.)

Amanda: "Her dad just died. I mean, I think we can cut
her a break."

Imelda: "She probably has a concussion."

Amanda: "She probably has five."

Imelda: "I thought she hated her dad."

Amanda: "Yeah. Always thought she hated her mom,
too."

Imelda: "Hey, I heard that she actually killed her dad. Like,
she was behind the wheel of the car. Ran him right over."

(A third set of footsteps joins them.)

Noor: "Will both of you please shut the hell up?"

There's a beep, the slide of a lock releasing and the door opens toward me. I'm already across the room with my headphones on, packing up my stuff. The three of them crowd the doorway.

"There you are," says Noor.

I don't like the way she's looking at me, not one bit. With pity, even though there's no reason to pity me. Out of all of them, I'm the winner. Me.

"Why did you disappear?" she asks. "There's a little press thing downstairs. They wanna talk to you."

I pull the headphones off my ears. "What?"

"Did you hear what I said?"

I can't look at any of them as they stand there, awkward and stupid around me for the first time ever. The fear in me hardens and turns into something mean, but I don't dare let them see it. Jason implied that I'm brain-dead or something, and much as I want to say everyone's crazy, what if they're not?

"Nah," I say. "I didn't hear a thing."

At the press thing, there are cameras. I ask Amanda what I should say but she just sighs.

"What?"

"You know I lost my fight, right?" she says, with an unexpected burst of anger. "I'm not undefeated anymore, Trisha. For the first time in my life I lost, and now you're here asking me about press? You think I'm invincible or something?"

She's taken her braids out and her hair is a dark halo around her head. She looks thinner, tired, less like a legend with every second that passes. I've never seen her like this, and I wonder about everything it took for her to be the star at our gym.

"I guess I never thought . . . I'm sorry."

"If Kru asks, I'm going for another walk," she says. I watch her leave and it shakes me because I've never seen her look so sad.

The cameras flash. I manage to say a couple things to the almost bored reporters there. They're not interesting things.

"Yeah."

"It was hard."

"I dunno."

I find a couple of smiles and they make me feel better when I start, so I smile some more. I forget about the things Amanda and Imelda were saying at the door of our hotel room, forget all the ways I got hit today. I smile and smile and everything is the way I imagined it. Now I know what it feels like to be a winner. For once, I'm in control.

It's better than any other feeling in the world.

✖

I try to stay awake on the flight back to Toronto but I'm so tired I fall asleep on Kru's shoulder. He's somehow sensed the distance between me and the other girls but thinks it's because I won a belt and they didn't. I don't correct him. I don't say: *It's because they think I'm crazy and maybe they're right because there's a soucouyant living in my house that looks a hell of a lot like my mother.*

You just can't say stuff like that to Kru.

I wake when the plane touches down. The force of the landing sucks me back into the seat and I feel that pull in every muscle in my body. When I try to stand to get my bag from the overhead compartment, I realize that all my strength is gone.

"I'll get that," Kru says. He seems sad, even though I won. We won. "Go on ahead."

"Thanks, Kru."

I turn back in the aisle and watch him grab the belt from above. I take the bag from him, but not the gaudy belt. "That's for the gym," I say. On the shelves with the other belts, above the training mats where everyone can see what you've earned. How you've made Kru proud. Except he doesn't seem all that proud right now, and I don't know what to say to him.

He pats my shoulder and tries to smile at me. I try to smile back, but this only makes him sadder.

The others look everywhere but at me, and in the airport bathroom, I see why. Coarse strands of hair have escaped my braid and are standing almost on end, fighting their way to the ceiling, but that's nothing compared to the damage done to my face. The bandages plastered over my nose are covered in droplets of blood. My eyes are pinpricks, shining out from dark hollows, and there's a cut on my lip that I haven't seen before. Now I'm aware of it, it starts to throb. I push into it with my fingertips and come away with blood under my nails. I push and push and push until there's no more blood.

I leave the airport without saying bye to any of them. I see Kru wave Noor off as he stands in arrivals, looking around for someone. On the bus to the train station, I realize he might have been looking for me, and I feel ashamed because I don't want to worry Kru. But not so ashamed I turn on my phone to call him.

By the time I get home, it's dark. I slip around back, skirting the parking lot. There are too many lights on in our unit, which means that Ma is home. I stand in the dark for so long I'm almost asleep on my feet, and maybe I am, because I don't hear Columbus calling my name until he's right in front of me.

"Holy shit," he says, pulling me under the streetlight.

I flinch and shake him off. "What the fuck happened to your face, Trisha?"

I grin wide, little firecrackers of pain bursting across my face, sending stars shooting behind my eyes. "I won a belt."

"Your mom is going to kill you," he says, then frowns at the look that crosses my face, the one I can't help, the one that says I'm so frightened I'd rather stand here in the dead of the night than go inside and face her. Columbus takes my hand and leads me to his house, through the back door and up the stairs and into his bedroom, where he sits me on his bed, takes off my shoes and gives me a glass of water with two Tylenols. He turns off the light so that he doesn't have to look at me any longer.

"I think I have a concussion," I say sleepily.

"Yeah, no kidding."

"I won, though, Christopher. I know I did. Wait, maybe it was a tie."

"You know it doesn't matter, right? And stop calling me Christopher. It doesn't sound like you."

"I killed my father."

He sighs. "It was an accident, Trish."

I try to push myself up on my elbows, try to peer at him in the darkness, but my elbows won't hold me up. I'm numb all over. I fall back onto the bed and blink up at him.

"Do you ever miss your dad?" I ask.

He shakes his head. "No. I'm glad he's gone."

"Me too."

"Go to sleep," he says, sounding older than he is. Older than me, which never happens. He pulls the covers over me and lowers his voice to a whisper so low I barely hear it. "You're my best friend, you know."

He hesitates and I think he's about to say something else, but he doesn't. He leaves the room. I feel his absence, feel the cold take hold of my body, then I fall asleep.

thirty-three

Rain on galvanized roofing. Pansticks on hammered steel. Liquid rhythms so loud that for a moment I think I'm in Trinidad, but I realize I'm in Columbus's bed and the music is coming from the other side of the wall, in my room.

Ma. She's calling to me.

I'm still numb from painkillers, feeling just fine. I slip downstairs, past Columbus on the couch. I don't wake him. Pammy is in her kitchen, singing softly to herself, gold glinting at her wrists. There's no trace of chamomile anywhere because she's in a boxed-wine kind of mood tonight. She's turned away from me, doesn't see me, so I back away and continue my journey down.

In bare feet, I cross from their front door to ours. It's unlocked.

I know I'll find her in the kitchen, so that's where I look first. But it's not her calling me. It's someone else.

"Where you been, girl?" says Ravi, from behind me.

I turn slowly. I didn't expect to see him. Columbus said he disappeared. I guess I'd hoped he was gone for good.

He's staring at me without seeing me at all. There are tears in his eyes, but I can't tell if they're from grief or anger. Maybe a bit of both and as soon as I realize that, he takes a step toward me. He's got the envelope in his hand. The one I left for him, with the insurance papers inside.

"You were supposed to kill my dad, weren't you, Ravi? In Trinidad, and here, too. You broke in here through the back door and there was supposed to be an accident, right? But he was late and we were coming home. Then he got hit by the car. But you were the one who was supposed to do it."

It's like he's not even hearing me. He's off in his own world. "Take money from me? Like I ain't been with you from the start? From when we was little kids?"

It takes me a minute to realize it's not me he's seeing, it's her.

He thinks I'm Ma.

"I almost kill a man for you," he says, and the tears stream down his face now. "I woulda done it, too. Before you did it yourself."

There's a possessiveness about him that's so much like how my dad used to look at Ma.

An expression on his face that tells me he isn't ever going to leave her.

That he did it for love, attacking Dad in Trinidad, pretending to break into the house and "surprise" Dad the night everything went wrong. When he found Dad drunk in the parking lot instead, in the moments before our car came smashing through the darkness.

Ravi did it out of love but for Ma there were other reasons, reasons that had nothing to do with him. I think about the bruise on her hip I saw when Dad came up from Trinidad that last time and, you know, I can't help but think about all the other bruises I'd been seeing on her my whole life.

My ma, she's had it rough.

Now what I see is the anger cloudy in his eyes and it's like he can tell what I'm thinking, that I need to get away somehow. He's as thin as I am, but slower, because when he reaches to grab me, I slip the bird bones of my hands out of his grip and am down the stairs, running. I feel him behind me as I wrench the door open but pull my bones through his hands again and feel a flare of triumph at my little wrists that can do this, that can slip out of these kinds of traps.

There's a car coming down the lane toward me, headlights bright in my eyes. Is that Ma? I can't tell.

I don't know what makes me do this, turn and run the other way, but I do. Right into the woods behind the parking lot. I just want to get away.

And I think, for a moment, that I'm free. So I stop because my head is spinning. I blink, but everything is hazy. The tree bark is cool against my temple.

I forget where I am and instead replay the events of my tourney fights. Didn't I relive a fight at Dad's funeral, too? It's what I do when my mind goes blank. Then I hear Ravi's voice in my head, him saying things to me as though I'm Ma. As if I'd ever do the things to him that Ma did. It wasn't enough for Ma to take everything from me, she had to drag Ravi into it, too.

There's light somewhere behind me and I remember a car pulling into the lot. Someone's calling my name but I don't want to be near anyone right now. I just want to stand here in the dark until morning comes. My phone rings, the sound shattering the quiet around me.

It's Jason. "Hello?" Jason says, his voice sounding groggy. "Trish, are you there? You butt-dialed me."

"Come get me," I whisper.

"Where are you? Trish? I'm at my parents' place. I can get the car from my dad and drive over in no time. Are you at home?" He's so freaked out he's tripping all over his words, tripping all over mine as I try to answer. I guess I sound as terrified as I feel.

I'm about to say yes, I'm at home, but a noise stops me. It doesn't feel like I'm alone anymore. Jason's speaking again, messing with my concentration so I hang up the phone.

Looking around, I don't see anybody, but I feel them.

I feel *him*.

Ravi isn't behind me, until he is. I didn't know he could move like that. With all the drugs Ma's been giving him he *shouldn't* be able to move so fast.

He puts his hands on my shoulders and I can't slip through this time. I spin, quickly. My hip lifts and torques and my right knee whips into his groin. He screams and falls, taking me with him to the dirt, pinning me there. We're close to the edge of the ravine, almost too close for me to maneuver properly, but I manage to buck him off, push and scrape my body from under him. I'm thanking Imelda now, and the BJJ she introduced us to. My ground game isn't great, but it's better than Ravi's.

Keep running, I think. *You're too fast for him.*

His hands close over my ankle and he pulls me back. I kick out—

and this is what it's like, when all your strength has deserted you and you know the punishment is coming, you know you're done, all glory lost in this one moment that you weren't good enough

—but right then I hear a sound, a whoosh of breath, a fierce cry that seems to rise from the earth, a wind whistling through the trees, falling like a hammer from the sky and it's everywhere at once this sound.

It's all around me.

It's Ma.

She's here with us and her hands are on Ravi. For a moment it looks like she's hugging him but no, that's not it. She's *pushing* him. Ravi's hands melt away and I smell her breath, metallic and full of blood, before I realize she's still screaming, even as she falls down into the ravine, bringing Ravi with her, and now her screams turn from anger to triumph before they die out.

Rain on galvanized roofing. Pansticks on hammered steel. The sound of bones breaking. A skull cracking apart.

thirty-four

Their bodies are twisted, broken. Ravi's neck is facing a direction it shouldn't be. His eyes are wide open and blood spews from his mouth. He sputters, chokes.

I'm about to go down to them but I feel a hand on my arm, anchoring me to the spot. "Wait," says Pammy.

We watch the blood spill from his mouth to the soil, and a kind of stillness overtake him.

Pammy takes her hand away. "It's safe now."

I hear her on the phone, calling the police. Her calm is gone, she sounds frantic. She's sobbing again, the same way she'd been the night my dad died. It feels like that night all over again, except worse. The sound of her voice grows distant as I scramble down the side of the ravine, step carefully around Ravi and go to Ma. I sit beside her and take her dirt-streaked hand into mine. "Ma," I say, "wake up."

I close my eyes and put my arms around her. That power of hers is gone, the one that came with the night, the one that turned her into a shrieking thing, fire personified, when Ravi dared put his hands on me.

And now, the night fades away and she's going, too.

The rising sun burns the outside of my lids until I force them open, see her clearly in the morning light. Her skin dry as paper, hair like coarse brush scattered around her head, a dry halo fit for kindling. The light hits it and for a moment it turns red, like it's alive. It's my concussion talking, the bone shard in my brain, maybe, because what I think in this moment is she's going to burst into flames and go shooting across the sky.

I notice for the first time that her eyes are open. I don't know how long she's been watching me. "My baby," she says, her voice rattling out from deep inside her chest. "I heard you calling me. They say there's a light in the tunnel, but there's no light. It was only dark. So dark. And then I heard your voice like it was when you were a little girl. My baby."

I don't even flinch when her hand finds mine, her fingers wrapping around my palm and squeezing with a strength I never thought would be possible, her on the ground like this, broken into pieces.

"Yes," I say, brushing the dirt from her hair. "Yours. Always yours."

"Trish? Is it safe now?" I look up at Pammy, who's watching over us from the top of the ravine. She's done with the phone-sobbing. Her tears dry and her calm returns. "Can I come down?"

"Yeah." I echo her from mere moments ago. "It's safe now."

Pammy picks her way carefully down the side of the ravine and sits cross-legged next to me. She takes Ma's other hand in hers and presses a kiss to the back of it.

thirty-five

The hospital is cold, so Jason has lent me his sweater. He showed up at my house after the cops arrived and hasn't really left me since. He's here now, sleeping beside me in the waiting room.

I put my head on his shoulder and close my eyes. When Aunty K finds us, we're holding hands. Pammy must have called her right after she called 9-1-1 because sometime in the last couple hours she hopped on a plane from New York and all of a sudden she's at the hospital with us. Maybe it's not all of a sudden. Maybe we've been here for a while and Pammy has been wrapped around me like a shield, sending cops and nurses and nosy busybodies catapulting away like she's electricity personified. She tried to send Jason away, too, but he refused to go.

"Can I speak to you for a minute, Trisha?" Aunty K asks.

Jason looks at me. "Want me to go, Trish?"

I don't really want to talk to her, but I know I have to. "No, it's okay. We'll go." I follow Aunty K out of the room. I see Jason staring at us through the glass doors.

She sees him, too. "Pammy says your boyfriend won't leave. What does he know about what happened?"

"Nothing. Pammy told me what to say to everyone."

"And the cops?"

"Haven't talked to them yet."

She looks relieved. Her hair is loose around her shoulders and there's a kind of determination about her that reminds me of Ma. "Good. Let's go over it again."

"Do we have to?"

"Yes! This is the story."

She tells it to me, almost word for word what Pammy said. They must have talked about it at some point.

"Are you listening?" Aunty K says, when it becomes clear I'm not.

I force myself to pay attention. This is where the important part comes in. I know this from experience.

Ravi was an addict. He wandered. Was off his head a lot. Ma must have gone looking for him and saw him at the bottom of the ravine there. Must have slipped on her way down. You came back from your tournament and saw their cars, but not them. Found them like that. When you got down there, Ravi was already dead.

Me, frowning: "It's a short story."

Pammy interrupts. She's brought some coffee for Aunty K. "Those are the ones that'll stick. Overdose on meds? Happens a hundred times a day. Besides, he's been addicted to painkillers since his warehouse accident, everyone could see that. Your Ma suspected it, at least, but she didn't want to believe something like that about her childhood sweetheart."

Aunty K nods at her. They're nodding at each other. Jason is watching us from the waiting room. Columbus is asleep. Ma is still broken.

"A tragedy," says the cop, when he finds us. He's looking at me for signs that I think maybe it's not. I can feel Aunty K and Pammy behind me, their stillness, their intense focus. Their faces twisted in grief, their eyes saying, yes, yes it's such a tragedy and everyone here thinks so.

He nods at the bandages on my nose, the bruises on my face. "That happened in your kick-boxing tournament?"

"Yeah, I had three fights. I won a belt."

"Where's the belt now?"

I can see it's a trick question, that he's trying to trip me up. Thinks maybe that I'm the weak link. So I give him Kru's number and tell him he can find the belt at the gym tomorrow, probably. He can find the tournament results online, too, if he wants.

"She even spoke to the press," Jason says. "There are videos online." He puts a hand on my shoulder. It seems like such a long time ago. It seems like another lifetime. I wonder how he knew about the videos but then realize he must have seen them on the gym's social media. Everyone knows everything these days. Except for what really goes on behind the scenes.

"I'm going to need a minute with your girlfriend," the cop says.

Jason doesn't blink at me being called his girlfriend. He squeezes my hand and walks away. I catch Pammy's eye, then Aunty K's.

Where the tears come from, I don't even know, but now they're falling from my lashes and the cop softens and in that moment we have him, we really do.

It's such a good story.

six months later

thirty-six

I think of rain on galvanized roofing.

The sun warms my back as I pass my hands over her hair, fingers combing coconut oil through the strands that have turned solid gray over the past few months. I turn the wheelchair so she can feel some of the heat, too. We've moved out of our townhouse and the new ground-floor apartment we're in gets a lot of light. She closes her eyes to the sensation and falls asleep. Since the accident, being wheeled into the warmth is what she loves the best. I guess when you're paralyzed from the waist down, you take whatever you get.

"You're so gentle with her. Such a good daughter," Pammy says from the doorway. She's staring at me in that new way of hers. Trying to see what I know, what I'll say, if I'll stick to the story, if she needs to call Aunty K.

She doesn't need to worry. The story is as much mine as it is hers, Ma's and Aunty K's.

The story is ours.

She doesn't shift from the doorway, seems content to call to me from just inside the room. "Christopher tells me you're focused on school now. You don't even go to the gym anymore."

"I don't have time with university and everything." It's only part of the truth. The fight in me is gone. It died the night I stood with Pammy up on the lip of the ravine and watched Ravi fall asleep for the last time. I've tried to go back to training, but it doesn't feel the same. Nothing will ever feel the same again. "Aunty K is coming for Christmas this year. Will you be around?"

"Of course." She smiles at me. "We have to be there for each other, especially in times like this."

When Pammy leaves, I separate Ma's hair into two sections and braid both, leaving a little tail hanging over each shoulder.

She wakes, putting a hand over mine. You can see how much she's aged in the new lines on her face, carving deep furrows at the corners of her mouth and eyes. You can hear it in her voice when she asks, panicked, "Where did you go?"

"Nowhere, Ma. I'm right here."

"Tell me about Junior," she says. She's been doing this a lot. Ever since she woke up from the accident, she's been encouraging me to reach out to Junior. I think it's because she's scared that if she dies, I'll be alone. I tell her all about him working at the garage. About him postponing uni for another year so that he can make some more money right now. She nods and tells me that sometimes you have to do that.

But she's made sure that I don't, and that my tuition is paid up.

"Sometimes I close my eyes and I see you win that fight. You know the one where you got a belt?"

I pitch my voice low, to match hers. No abrupt movements. No sharp noises. There's only infinite gentleness for her now. "Yeah, I remember. But it was a tie. A split decision."

"No, you won, baby. I saw it with my own eyes." I don't know if she did. I don't know if she was ever there, or if we'd both imagined her in Florida. She finally notices the fresh braids and nudges one of them with her chin. "Your father loved the smell of coconut in my hair," she says, her lids falling closed again.

"Ma," I say. "Why did Ravi have Dad's phone?"

"Mmmm . . ." Ma sighs. She's almost in that dream-state, the one she enters into most afternoons, and into the evening. Maybe that's why her accent comes back strong. "Your father dropped it that night, when they fight. Ravi picked it up after. He wasn't supposed to. He should have just left it on the ground."

It was the last thing I didn't know. But, you know, I'm not sure what difference answers make. With Ravi and Dad dead. Ma like this, a black widow who can't even move her legs.

She falls silent. I think she's asleep when she hits me with this: "I know you didn't mean to kill him. You were driving, it was dark."

"There was rain," I remind her.

"Yes," she nods. "The rain. But you hadn't seen him. You didn't mean to."

My hand on the wheel of the car and, suddenly, her hand on mine.

Outside, two shadows, one seeming to freeze the moment before it disappears into the woods, the other stepping away from the car.

Away or toward?

Does it matter?

A slight bend of pressure on the wheel.

Her or me?

Doesn't matter.

I wait until I'm sure she's asleep again before I press a kiss to her head and rub some warmth into her shoulders and pull some of her heat into my hands. My ma, she's had it so rough. Now I hope she gets to be a little bit easy. "Yes, I really did."

I put some money in her purse, not because she needs it, but because she likes to know there's a little extra in there just in case. Then I leave before the weak fall sun sets behind the trees. Leave before she gives herself to the night, sheds the skin of her broken body, a body she broke for me, hers, and becomes fire.

In her dreams or mine? Does it—

thirty-seven

It's all coming back now.

It had been raining that whole day, with thunderstorms in the forecast for the evening. When your aunt who can't keep her mouth shut showed up to sweep you off to dinner; she was late coming in from the airport because of the weather.

No amount of protesting could stop what was inevitable.

When your Ma who can't keep her legs together gives you that look (you know, *that* one) it's all over for you. You're to be squeezed into a narrow table at the hakka place on the other side of town, listening to them gossip about people they used to know back home and the particulars of running a roti shop in this economy. There is complete disgust at the endless appetites of Trinidadians. You can't get away with small roti, uh-uh. They must be large and filled to bursting or else the pot-bellied diaspora will turn on you in a second. There's some discussion about the diabetes epidemic sweeping the island. You secretly agree that it's not undeserved. You wish for a level of self-awareness about the connection to diabetes and the sodium / fat / sugar-laden food you're about to eat, but the moment for that passes with the rumbling of your stomach.

You order hakka chow mein and vegetable balls in hot garlic sauce and hope there's enough nutrition in the meal to feed your muscles, make them sturdier, stronger. The meal is strangely tense. Ma and Aunty K keep up the chatter, but their attention isn't in the room with you, so you tune out and let your mind wander. They don't say anything about your lack of participation, and don't seem to mind in particular.

This is what you remember most about that night. It was meant to be a spontaneous gesture, a fun dinner with your kooky aunt, but everyone was acting strangely and you were feeling a bit ill. There's some mild heartburn after dinner but you insist it's nothing as the three of you duck under a single umbrella and sprint to the car.

Raindrops, yeah, but not on galvanized roofing. You'll wonder at it much later, how the musical quality of rain deserted you on that night and you didn't even notice. The chatter continues into the car, but it's only Aunty K this time. There's an attempt at the radio but Ma's nerves can't take it, so she switches it off and you're left with the sound of heat whooshing through the air vents and a voice that's easily drowned out.

Ma's phone rings and because you're next to her, you hear Pammy's voice on the other end, shrill, as if in warning, before Ma gives you an annoyed look out of the corner of her eye and shifts her body so you can't hear anymore. Whatever Pammy says upsets her. It has something to do with Dad. He's not home yet, or something, and maybe that's a problem. He's late. Her hands shake before she pulls them away. Squeezes one in the other, a silent bid to stay calm, then returns them to her knee.

When you pull onto the road to your townhouse co-op, when you're about to turn into the parking lot, one of those hands shoots out, grabs the steering wheel . . .

To what? Help you? Stop you?

You're driving, but the both of you turn the wheel.

The both of you steer the car into the drunk man stumbling around the parking lot.

You both killed your father.

Both wanted him dead.

You walk now, through the university campus.

Your boyfriend, Jason, has his arm around you. The two of you are closer now, ever since he showed up at the hospital to help you get through what was happening with your Ma. He's been so sweet, and you finally know what good dick is. You've also begun to hate that term and love reggaetón. He's forgiven you for everything because of what you were going through at home. He's a really good guy.

You think he loves you, even though you're not a fighter anymore. You think he loves you *because* you're not a fighter anymore.

Maybe you are, just a different kind.

After he leaves to go study, you walk alone.

You didn't go to Ryerson like you thought you would. You decided on the University of Toronto, because you miraculously got in and you think it's a better school. That's what everyone says, anyway. And you like walking through this pretty downtown campus. You're going to do business management regardless, so why not do it somewhere with nicer buildings and lots of green space. Somewhere so big you can be anonymous. Just a face in the crowd. Surrounded by throngs of students who look just like you.

No one will recognize you here.

You get to be a person without a past, and that's for the best, isn't it? Because what's real about the past, anyway? You don't know. Maybe you never will.

What you do know:

Your father's face.

A story that ends with a thud.

A shadow slipping into the woods.

It was a dark, rainy night. Moonless,
and thank God for that.

A slide out of a nightmare.

the end

acknowledgments

I acknowledge the Indigenous territories upon which I live and work.

Thank you to Lynne Missen, Georgia Murray, Peter Phillips, Sam Wiebe, Sunni Westbrook and David Pledger for their feedback and hard work in helping me bring this book to life. Also to David Chariandy for his wonderful novel *Soucouyant*, which provided so much inspiration.

Some creative liberties regarding the sport of Muay Thai were taken to make the story work, and all errors belong to me and the voices in my head. I would like to extend special thanks to Sr. Kru Yai Michael Perez of Southside Muay Thai in Toronto for introducing me to Muay Thai some twenty years ago, and for training me for the past ten. No teacher deserves to be cursed with a willful and stubborn student such as myself, but he has done what he could with the little he's been given.

I am grateful for the women of Trinidad, who have sustained me all these years with their love and, let's be honest, their delicious cooking. I do not deserve even a fraction of the effort, but I'm going to eat their food anyway because the alternative (my cooking) is too sad to contemplate.

Finally, this book is dedicated to Darryl and Andre, who are the best brothers in the entire history of brothers. They make me want to be a better sister. Hypothetically.

xx Sheena